"Kiss me again, Christianna."

Nate bent his head once more and acknowledged the need. For fulfillment in her, yes. Definitely that. But for other things, too. Undefined things that even now threatened him in ways he couldn't comprehend.

"Nate." Just his name, breathed out on the same kind of sexy little sigh that had tortured him once before.

Her response made him crazy and his imagination went wild. He pictured them together at his cottage, making love night after night.

Except Nate didn't do *night after night,* with all it entailed. It was too easy to forget it in her arms. He fought for sanity. Fought to keep from losing himself. From free-falling into something that came as close to scaring him as anything could.

JENNIE ADAMS

Australian author Jennie Adams grew up in a rambling farmhouse surrounded by books, and by people who loved reading them. She decided at a young age to be a writer, but it took many years and a lot of scenic detours before she sat down to pen her first romance novel. Jennie is married with two adult children, and has worked in a number of careers and voluntary positions, including transcription typist and preschool assistant. Jennie makes her home in a small inland city in New South Wales. In her leisure time she loves long, rambling walks, starting knitting projects that she rarely finishes, chatting with friends, trips to the movies and new dining experiences

Jennie Adams also writes for the
Harlequin Romance® line—so if you
like Chrissy and Nate's story, look out for
Jennie's upcoming titles...coming soon!

Her
Millionaire
Boss

JENNIE ADAMS

SILHOUETTE *Romance*

Published by Silhouette Books

America's Publisher of Contemporary Romance

 SILHOUETTE BOOKS

ISBN-13: 978-0-373-19835-1
ISBN-10: 0-373-19835-3

HER MILLIONAIRE BOSS

First North American Publication 2006

Visit Silhouette Books at www.eHarlequin.com

Printed in U.S.A.

Dear Reader,

Like Chrissy Gable in this book, I enjoy growing plants and flowers—and, like Chrissy, I meet with mixed success. My latest gardening projects include six strawberry plants yielding lovely fruit—and two producing brown blobs—and a small flower garden, which I confess looks better since my daughter took over most of its care.

I love to hear from readers, and can be contacted through my Web site at www.jennieadams.net

Jennie Adams

For Mark, because my world needs your light.
For my children, my treasures always.
And for "the bats"—you know who you are.

CHAPTER ONE

'YOU'RE not going into Henry's sick room, Margaret. Not like this.' Not with a lawyer at her side and greed all over her face.

Chrissy Gable took a deep breath of antiseptic-laden hospital air, and looked her boss's second wife right in her calculating eyes. 'His health is too precarious to risk upsetting him. Surely you can understand that?'

With her heart pounding hard, Chrissy faced the other woman. Even the usual weight of waist-length hair bundled onto her head and bound with a couple of chopsticks felt leaden at this moment. If Margaret had cared even the slightest bit for her elderly husband's health...

Instead, she had delayed her return to Melbourne until the end of her vacation at Mount Selwyn. Why let duty interfere with her fun?

Henry didn't deserve a wife like Margaret. He hadn't deserved to be deserted by his grandson six years ago, either.

Nate Barrett had transferred to the overseas arm of the company just weeks before Chrissy had commenced working for Henry. The man had shucked his grandfather off like excess baggage, even though Henry had all but raised him as a son.

Chrissy had wondered if her boss would ever get over the

hurt. Henry may have been recently married, but Nate's leaving had shredded the older man's heart. Chrissy had made it her task to help her boss through the pain. She and Henry had formed a deep bond. She would watch over him now, too.

'Get out of my way,' Margaret grated.

I don't think so. Margaret might have tricked Henry long enough once to get a ring on her finger. He might now be too proud, gentlemanly or inexplicably smitten to cast the fifty-year-old off.

To Chrissy's mind, however, the woman lacked decidedly in redeeming features. 'Lose the lawyer, and I'll be happy to move.'

'I'm Henry's wife.' Margaret's hands curled into fists. 'I have every right—'

'Every right to what? Upset him? Cause a second stroke that could be fatal?' Did Margaret's greed know no bounds? 'He's too ill to deal with a lawyer right now, so I suggest you take your Power of Attorney form and—'

'How do you know…?' Margaret broke off and pushed forward. 'Out of my way. You're just his secretary.'

The man at her side followed.

'It's PA, actually, and I'm not shifting.' Chrissy held her ground in front of the closed door of the hospital room but her nerves screamed. She couldn't let Margaret coerce Henry into signing anything. Nor could she allow the woman to have Henry declared mentally unfit.

She had to stop this, but how? One thought formed. Desperately, she snatched at it. 'Henry came around. Was completely lucid. Earlier. While I sat with him.'

A guilty heat stole into her face at the fib, but oh, how she wished it could be true. 'He's perfectly capable of looking after his own affairs.'

'That's a lie.' Margaret leaned forward, her thin mouth

pinched. 'He's been as good as a vegetable since they brought him here yesterday.'

Righteous anger roared through Chrissy at Margaret's callous attitude. 'If I'd started work for him just a few months earlier, I'd have stopped you ever getting your snares...' She broke off. 'You seem to think you know an awful lot about his condition, for someone who's only just arrived.'

'A nurse—' Margaret clamped her lips shut, but Chrissy got the picture. Margaret had wasted no time in ensuring she had a spy in the place.

'Mrs Montbank has rights,' the lawyer announced. 'You are attempting to stand in the way of her exercising those rights.'

'*Mr* Montbank has rights, too.' Forget the slimy legal eagle, she thought, and instead she turned to Margaret again. 'I repeat, I won't let you in. You just want to shove Henry into Assisted Care and go your merry way, spending all his money.'

'How dare you?' Air hissed through Margaret's clenched teeth. The truth of Chrissy's accusations filled her eyes. 'What do you know? Who's told you—?'

'Mrs Montbank.' The lawyer stepped forward. 'Let me handle this.'

'Don't bother.' Chrissy spread herself before the closed door. Feet apart. Arms out. In the most threatening manner she could manage, she waggled her head and deployed the only defence she had. 'Observe the headgear. Those are real porcelain chopsticks in there. I'll use them if I have to!'

Margaret almost laughed, then her eyes narrowed. 'Are you threatening me?'

'I simply know that Henry would never willingly give you control of anything more than your budgeted allowance, Margaret—not of his personal funds, and certainly not of his business dealings. I'll testify to it if I have to.'

'You little tramp.' Fury radiated from Margaret. 'You're probably sleeping with him, hoping to take him from me.' She raised a clawed hand.

Now, *that* was too much. *How dared Margaret insult Henry that way?* How dared she insult Chrissy's relationship with her boss? Without conscious thought, Chrissy raised her arm toward the buried chopsticks.

'Thanks for holding the fort while I got some air, sweetheart.' A man strode toward the group. Tall. Compelling. Effortlessly confident.

His turbulent blue gaze locked with hers. 'Showing off your hairstyling abilities again, huh?'

He gave an indulgent grin that didn't reach his eyes. 'You shouldn't dislodge those valuable antique chopsticks though, babe. What if you dropped one and it shattered?'

Babe? Sweetheart? Antique chopsticks? Who was this man? He made absolutely no sense. Yet the tone of his voice, the slight caress in it, the height and breadth and *strength* of him, all swamped her senses.

Muted sounds of hospital, of metal trolleys on polished floors, of professionals conferring in lowered tones dimmed. She saw only the man before her. Heard only her heartbeat, drumming her confusion and awareness.

When the warning in his gaze gave way to sensual heat, she knew he felt the connection, too. Long moments of still, silent acknowledgement passed between them.

She didn't know this man, yet everything within her screamed that she did. That she had always known him, and would always know him.

'Missed me?' He clasped her raised arm, drew it up and around until her fingers speared into the crisp black hair at his nape. His hand covered hers, held it there as her anger subsided and confusion and awareness rose.

'Um, well—'

'Indeed.' One kiss on her forehead. Another pressed against the crease at the side of her mouth. A hint of lemon and ginger on his breath.

She tasted the flavour of it from the side of her mouth with her tongue.

His gaze followed the movement, darkened, then turned to warning as hot, firm lips moved to whisper into her ear. 'Your name?'

'Christianna. Chrissy. Gable. Chrissy Gable.' Or should that be Chrissy *Gabble*? Her thoughts struggled through the veil of weariness and stress. Struggled to come to terms with *him*.

This knight errant. This rescuer who had scorched her with a look and the barest of touches. Only one identity made any sense, but it couldn't be. No way would *he* have bothered to come back. When people left like that, they never returned. And she would never have this sort of feeling for—

'Ah. Henry's PA. I should have known.' Lean fingers traced across her skin with an exploratory insistence that belied the businesslike tone of his words.

Chrissy's eyelids drooped behind her glasses. Just when she thought she would give in to the call of her senses and tilt her face completely into his hand, he stopped and shifted away. Cleared his throat. Blanked his face into a mask of calm determination as he faced the tableau of lawyer and avaricious wife.

'Get rid of the lawyer, Margaret, as Chrissy has suggested. Then you can see Henry. Otherwise, there's nothing you can achieve here.'

Margaret puffed up angrily. 'He's my husband—'

'Yes. And he'll be watched over very carefully during every moment of his recovery. Do you understand?'

A look passed between him and Margaret. Burning anger on his part. Some other sort of burning on hers. Chrissy shivered at the impact of those clashing looks.

Margaret's hard stare glanced off her, and turned back to the man at her side. Shifted subtly into something else. 'You haven't even been in the country. What is she to you?'

He looked at Chrissy, looked back to Margaret. 'It's none of your business.'

'You didn't think that way once.'

'You're delusional.' He examined her face with a passionless look of his own.

Margaret looked as though she would like to say more, then clamped her mouth into an unflattering line. 'This isn't the end. I'll see my husband with a thousand lawyers, if I want to.' She spun and walked away, her companion silent at her side.

Chrissy reached for a businesslike approach to counteract the way this man had made her feel. Even now, she struggled to accept that he had brought out such reactions in her.

'You're Nate Barrett. Henry's grandson.' It was the only thing that made sense. No way would Margaret have given way to anyone else. Not even for a moment.

He inclined his head. 'I'm afraid you had the advantage over me at first.'

Despite what Chrissy might have thought of Nate Barrett in past years, despite how he had made her feel just now, he had to be informed. 'Margaret was trying to get Power of Attorney, or get Henry declared unfit. I'm not sure exactly which, but I doubt she would stop at much to get what she wants.'

The woman's greed was legendary. 'I discovered by accident that Henry put her on a budget twelve months ago, but her behaviour hasn't changed much. Except to reveal her bitterness. I hate to think what could happen if she got control within the company, or of Henry's personal funds.'

'She won't be allowed to try to get at him or his money again.' He said it with absolute conviction.

Chrissy could see the similarities to Henry now. Nate shared the tall stature, the breadth of shoulders. The Montbank stamp had honed his features into a strong, to-die-for appeal.

He doesn't hold a to-die-for appeal for me. He can't, because I know what he's really like. Who was she trying to convince, though? Besides herself?

The man abandoned his grandfather. Gave Henry years of heartache.

Why had he come? What had driven him? It couldn't be more than a momentary guilt. Her resolve to dislike him stiffened. 'Why did you pretend we're involved?'

'You do realise you were about to get yourself slapped with an assault charge? It doesn't matter whether you intend to actually harm a person or not. If the threat is there...' His mouth twitched. 'Even if it is a threat of attack by killer chopsticks. What would you have done? Poked her eye out with one?'

'Dear God.' Suddenly she wished she could sit down. 'I can't believe—'

'Hey.' The humour left his face. 'You've been under stress. I seriously doubt you'd have done her any harm.'

The stress might explain the chopstick idea. It didn't explain why she had stood passively while Nate Barrett had kissed her.

To him it had been an act, of course. A way to stop her from getting into trouble with Margaret's lawyer.

The surprise of it had got to her. That was why she hadn't resisted. Now resentment and anger flared afresh. She met those feelings with relief. How dared he stroll back here after years of absence and kiss his grandfather's PA just like that, anyway? 'Couldn't you have stopped me some other way?'

'I had limited time and no idea who you were.' Chrissy

Gable had asked a simple question, yet Nate didn't have a simple answer. Nothing had been simple since he got the message that his grandfather had suffered a stroke.

Wanting Chrissy was yet another complication. He didn't want to admit that touching her hadn't only been for the sake of expediency. 'It seemed the best way to get that arm away from your weaponry without drawing the lawyer's notice.'

A casual touch. Two simple kisses that should have meant nothing. Instead, that touch, those kisses, had started a slow burn in his gut. In truth, the burn had started the moment he'd locked gazes with her. And it hadn't stopped yet.

'I guess I should thank you, even if you've given Margaret the impression that we're close, and that I go around wearing priceless artefacts in my hair, instead of store-bought kitchen implements.' Chrissy's mouth pursed. 'I couldn't find anything else, you see, so I thought the chopsticks would do.'

He gave a cursory nod. Wondered if her lateral thinking extended to other areas of her life. Like her love life. His interest in her burned, but it wouldn't be wise to act on it.

Relationships—the ones that mattered—didn't work out for Nate. He had proved it first with his mother, then later with Henry. Nowadays, he preferred to be alone and to keep his involvements casual. It was the sensible choice.

Chrissy Gable didn't strike him as the casual type. 'Very inventive of you to raid the kitchen for hairdressing implements.'

'Sometimes innovation is the only way.' She toyed with the frames of her glasses.

His gaze roved over her. Nut-brown hair sat in a coronet of braids atop her head with the two chopsticks poking out at angles. A grey business suit clung to her slender body and made her eyes seem brighter.

Those eyes behind the enormous horn-rimmed glasses changed as he watched her. Chilled. She might have responded to him minutes ago, but she clearly didn't want to accept the attraction. It was more, even, than that. 'You've chosen not to like me, haven't you?'

'That's true. I don't like you.' Attraction aside, she clearly meant it. 'I also don't know that I can trust you with Henry, any more than I could trust Margaret. But you're the only hope I've got.'

'You have no choice but to trust me.' *I share the attraction, Chrissy Gable, and I wonder what we're going to do about that?*

The answer should be a clear-cut nothing, but he wanted to explore further. To test out these reactions they shared. A little curiosity never hurt anyone. So maybe he would test the waters. If he felt so inclined.

It was a choice, after all, not a necessity. 'Your distress call brought me. Did you think I wouldn't answer it when I received your message?'

Her face told him she had thought precisely that. And had damned him for it, for the years of absence.

It amazed him that he wanted to defend himself. What could he say?

When my grandfather's new wife turned up naked in my bed, I decided Australia wasn't big enough for the three of us and I left?

He had made the choice so Henry wouldn't have to know of Margaret's behaviour. Now he was back for a short time and uncertain of his reception. He certainly wasn't going to tell this prickly woman any of that! 'It's time I saw my grandfather.'

'I'll come with you.' She chewed on her lip, before saying grudgingly, 'Thank you for stopping me before. It's appreciated, but it doesn't mean I won't make you sorry if you upset Henry yourself.'

'He's awake? Lucid?' His heart thumped. In moments he

might be speaking to Henry. Would his grandfather look at him with those same wounded eyes that had begged an explanation Nate hadn't been able to give?

Six years ago, when Nate had made it clear he had to go and refused to say why, Henry had sold him the overseas arm of the company for a pittance. Had insisted Nate take it. Nate had tried to be generous in return, but Henry had refused to accept any money from the business Nate had turned into a multi-million-dollar concern.

Then, three years ago, Henry had asked Nate to come back. To share once more in the running of the business here. Henry had seemed almost desperate. Nate had told his grandfather he didn't want to make that step backward. 'You said he'd spoken—'

'I'm sorry. No. I made that up to try to keep Margaret at bay. He's disoriented.' Her mouth pursed into a ferocious moue. 'That's temporary. He'll be back to his normal self and tossing cryptic clues around the office again before we know it.'

'Clues about what?' He shook his head. It wasn't important. The only things that mattered were Henry's health, and keeping the company in good order. Those, Nate could work on. If Henry would trust him with them.

'Never mind. Look, if my grandfather's condition isn't temporary—'

'Of course your grandfather's condition is temporary.' She said it with such passion that his body hummed in response.

Unnerved, he raised an eyebrow, feigning an indifference he didn't feel. 'Surely nobody can be sure of that at this stage?'

'I don't understand why you would say such things. Henry *has* to get better. Completely better. I refuse to contemplate any other option.' On those heartfelt words, she opened the door of the hospital room, and entered.

Nate followed. His grandfather looked awful. Tubes and

monitors covered Henry. His long frame seemed defenceless beneath the hospital-issue linens. Henry appeared to have aged ten years since Nate had seen him, not six.

This sick, vulnerable man would never run a company again. Henry was seventy years old, should have retired years before. It hit Nate hard that he should have seen that need when Henry asked him to come back. He would never have returned here, but he should have made Henry agree to retirement.

'Gramps.' The word caught in his throat. Hadn't been used since Nate was a child and Henry had taken him in when his mother opted out.

Nate reached out a hand to touch Henry's where it lay against the covers. Without raising his gaze, he said in a low voice to Chrissy, 'Sit down. You're feeling the strain more than you realise.'

'How did you know?' She sat abruptly.

How *had* Nate known? He had simply intuited her feelings, had felt connected closely enough to her even at opposite sides of a hospital bed that he just knew.

'Surprised…you…came. No…need.' His grandfather's voice was slurred, his breath laboured, the words themselves full of the years of separation and hurt.

Nate closed his eyes and tried to block the pain. 'I had to come.'

I had to come, but I don't want to make things worse, so please don't think I'll stay past making sure you'll be OK.

Chrissy clutched Henry's other hand in hers. 'You're speaking. I've been so concerned. I'll look after everything at work. You don't need to worry—'

'I'll do it.' Nate spoke over her, over rash promises she couldn't possibly keep. His gaze sought his grandfather's. 'I'll make sure everything is taken care of.'

'Don't…need….' Henry stopped to draw a breath.

'You can trust me.' A muscle worked in Nate's jaw. 'I'll fix things so it's all right.'

Did his grandfather understand that he hadn't wanted to hurt him six years ago, or three years ago? That he never wanted to hurt him?

I can give you this much, Gramps. Help when you need it. It's all I have.

'I'm sure Nate's welcome to stay for a short time.' Chrissy's tone said the opposite, although her expression was bland enough. 'But *I* can manage in your absence. The important thing is that you be free of worry and stress. Your only focus should be to relax and get better.'

'I agree.' Nate kept his tone calm and even. 'But I'm more qualified to take control than your PA.'

'Run…own…blasted…business,' Henry grumped. 'Sign…out…today…if…wanted to.'

Chrissy's mouth trembled before she firmed it. At the sight, Nate's frustration drained away.

'You've had a stroke.' Her voice trembled, too, just the tiniest bit. 'If you don't look after yourself, it could happen again and the next one could be much worse.'

She took a deliberate deep breath, then leaned forward to whisper, 'Who'd test cryptic crossword clues on me then? Or take me out for lattes on Thursdays or argue with me about the different football teams?'

'I…like…the…footy.' Henry's mouth turned down.

Her voice softened to warm affection. 'We'll be watching the footy matches on your big-screen TV again before you know it.'

How close were his grandfather and his PA? Before Nate could consider the question, Henry turned his gaze toward him.

The tired eyes searched his for a long time, then softened,

the anger replaced by at least a tenuous acceptance. 'You…can…run things…until I'm better.'

That was all Nate needed to hear. He ignored the hint of further expectation in his grandfather's eyes. 'I'll make sure everything's all right. Meanwhile, you get some rest.'

On those words, he unfolded his long legs from the chair and stood. Chrissy's gaze followed his movements, tracked over his charcoal suit and matching shirt.

Not once since he had entered the room and sat by his grandfather had he managed to completely banish her from his consciousness. Now his body tightened in awareness of her.

A nurse glanced in at the door. 'How are we doing?'

'Henry's making sense.' A tiny dimple flirted with Chrissy's right cheek. 'He woke up and we had a talk. His speech was slow but lucid.'

'Brilliant.' The nurse's smile was bright, winsome. It didn't do a thing for Nate. 'I'll let his doctor know.'

'Get well, Henry.' Chrissy kissed his resting form, then stepped back.

Henry stirred slightly.

Nate squeezed the old man's hand. 'I'll speak to your doctor about having you shifted out of here. The security's not tight enough for my liking.'

Chrissy opened her mouth as though to question him. He gave a slight shake of his head, put his hand to the small of her back and eased her out the door.

'Not here.' He growled the words into her ear.

She shivered, and a reaction, warm and pleasurable, flowed through him.

A moment later, she stalked from the room. When they were far enough along the corridor that Henry couldn't possibly hear them, she turned toward him, her eyes the liquid hue of mercury. 'There's absolutely no need for you to be here for more than a day or two. I can handle things, like I said.

'And just where do you think you're going to move my boss, anyway?'

CHAPTER TWO

'HENRY will go into Acebrook Hospital. It's a small private hospital outside the city.' Nate spoke decisively from behind Chrissy.

She reached the end of the hospital corridor and opted for the flight of stairs instead of the lift. 'Just like that, you have the whole thing organised? What makes you so sure Acebrook is the right place for Henry?'

What gives you the right to make the decisions for him? You've been away for six years without appearing to give a damn.

Her reaction wasn't entirely rational. Nate seemed concerned with Henry's best interests now. But this man made her want him on the one hand, while she disapproved of him thoroughly on the other.

Was it any wonder her feelings were divided about his care of Henry, too? 'And if you had Acebrook in mind, why didn't you mention it to Henry? Surely he deserved a say in his own care?'

'My grandfather had exhausted himself.' Assurance blazed on his face. 'I saw no reason to burden him with something I could take care of myself.'

Grudgingly, she said, 'I've heard of Acebrook.'

'Then you'll know it caters to a lot of celebrities. Their security measures go beyond the norm. Wife or not, Margaret won't be allowed to upset him there.'

Henry *could* get better faster somewhere like that, and that was all that mattered in the end. 'Margaret will demand to see him, no matter where he is.'

'I'll take care of that.' Again, just simple fact. 'A group of specialists will examine Henry to confirm his lucidity. Then *my* team of lawyers will inform Margaret's that my grandfather has deputised me to operate the company in his absence. Margaret will realise she has no power to do anything other than wish her husband a speedy recovery.'

'Henry only verbally said you could—'

'Actually, the authority was arranged years ago. Just in case of an emergency.' His words brushed, almost physically, across the back of her neck.

'Oh.'

'As for Margaret…' His lip curled. 'Provided her visits are in a controlled environment, she can go right ahead and play the loving wife.'

'I'd like to see that.' The back of Chrissy's neck still tingled. For once she wished she had her hair down, to protect the vulnerable skin at her nape. Since she didn't, she took the coward's way out and increased her pace to put some distance between them.

Nate cleared his throat, then launched into further speech. 'I realise you must be exhausted. I'd like to let you go home to sleep, but I could use your help today at the office. Can you manage?'

His thoughtfulness took her unawares. He wasn't supposed to be nice, not even some of the time. She had been so certain he wouldn't be.

'My sisters sat with Henry earlier while I went home to shower and change. I can manage my work day.'

'Thanks.' His gaze roamed her face. The secrets in the depths of his eyes made her skin heat and her heart flutter. Had he just visualised her in that shower?

Why would a man of the world like Nate Barrett harbour more than a momentary interest in her?

He blinked, and whatever she had seen disappeared behind a wall of determined resolve. 'I'd like to address a couple of issues before we arrive at work.'

See? Banished from his thoughts just like that. Why couldn't *she* do likewise about *him*?

Then she noted the aggressive tone of his voice. Her instincts prickled and she unconsciously straightened her spine. 'What issues?'

'If you're a power tripper,' he growled, 'if you intend to be difficult while I'm in charge of things—'

'I am certainly *not* a power tripper.' Had he really thought that? *Put the shoe on your own foot, bozo!* If anyone gave off the attitude of demanding to be in control, it was Nate.

She, on the other hand, aside from the tiny problem of not being able to ignore his effect on her, was at peace with herself. She didn't need to prove anything. To him or to anyone else. Her personal dragons had been slain, thank you very much.

Dragon-slaying aside, you don't want this man to hang around for weeks, getting underfoot and disturbing your peace. That doesn't make you controlling. It just makes you smart.

'I simply see no need for you to take over the running of the business when I can handle things myself while Henry gets better.'

'What experience do you have? What are your credentials? What training do you have in high-level management?' He fired the questions at her with the accuracy of a paint-ball champion. They hit and spread as quickly, undermining her shaky resolve. 'What if Henry's recovery takes months? What if it never happens?'

'He *will* get better. Totally better.' Henry was talking already. Surely that boded well for the future? 'As for the rest, I've worked closely enough with Henry that I know—'

'Watching isn't the same as doing.' His expression hardened, demanded that she accept his words. 'It's not enough. Not in the longer term.'

'For a week or two—'

'It'll be longer. You saw how he looked.'

She wanted to argue, but he was right, darn him. Still, accepting that fact didn't come easily. 'OK, so suppose you're right and his *complete recovery* takes longer. What happens?'

'I take care of things. It's what I told him back there, and I meant it.' His words brushed off her concerns like unwanted lint on his pristine suit. 'You'll co-operate with me? While I straighten things out here?'

'I'm surprised you're willing to stay indefinitely, but, provided your actions are in the best interests of the company, I'll do my best to support you.'

Who knew, she thought madly, maybe Nate would find a way to breathe new life into the company? Lately, she had begun to wonder if everything was OK. It was just a feeling, but—

'I didn't say I would be…' He left the thought unfinished. 'You said in your message that you were with Henry when the stroke happened. Do you usually work weekends?'

'It was a social outing.' She still felt guilty that her boss had been rambling through the treasure trove of Melbourne's retail side-streets with her when the stroke happened.

A pause. Then a rapped-out, 'Doing what?'

'Examining aged silk.' She could have explained about her

sister Bella's fetish for clothing design, but she doubted this man would be interested. 'Henry knows about stuff like that. I took him to look at a piece of fabric that I found in a back-street shop.'

When he didn't speak, she paused on the stairs, her gaze locked straight ahead. 'Do you have any more questions, or is the interrogation over?'

His silence lasted long enough that she gave in to curiosity and glanced over her shoulder. She had thought he might be holding his fire until they were face to face.

What she hadn't expected was to discover his gaze roving over her with undiluted interest. Even now, it lingered on her butt. Before she could tell him to stop looking at her most hated, far-too-large-in-her-opinion feature, he looked up, raw awareness in his eyes.

Any distance she had managed since they met disintegrated instantly. Forget his accusations, she decided frantically. They could wait until later. 'I think we should move right along to discussing how to manage the office while Henry is recovering!'

Surely that would be a safe topic. One that couldn't distract her into a molten mass of awareness of him. She turned her head frontward so fast she almost gave herself whiplash, then prayed he was no longer watching *The Barging of the Behemoth Bum* as she hurried down the rest of the stairs and pushed desperately at the exit door.

Fresh air. Thank God. She welcomed the sharp bite of the wind against her cheeks as she tried to reason out her reactions to him. 'Well? Don't you have anything to say about how we should tackle things in Henry's absence?'

'I have rather a lot to say about the way we should *tackle things*, actually.' His growled words brought her no comfort. The look in his eyes hinted that he wasn't thinking simply of the working relationship they would have to endure.

She stepped aside as a harried-looking woman passed them to enter the building. 'Good. About work, then.'

So what if that hadn't been all he meant? 'There are always crises at the company. We'll need to keep Henry informed, or he'll worry, but we'll make sure he understands that we're coping.'

After a pause, Nate nodded. 'There are things you don't understand, but, for now, one last question.'

'What is it?'

He leaned forward to touch a corkscrew curl that had escaped from her clump of braids.

Where was her ongoing antagonism toward him now? Her feet were frozen to the spot. She wanted very much to know what it would be like if he closed the distance between them and… Her breath hitched as he wrapped the curl around his fingertip, then let it spring free.

'Your glasses are fogging up,' he observed. 'Maybe you should take them off.'

The glasses were her shield. 'Oh, but my eyes—'

'Are a very lovely shade of grey. I can't help but wonder why you hide them.'

What big eyes you have, said the Wolf.

Wasn't that supposed to be Red Riding Hood's line?

'Uh.' They stood almost nose to nose. Nate's large body shielded her from the worst of the wind, and she liked the feeling that engendered. Liked his closeness and the size and strength of him.

Good grief. I don't want the Wolf to kiss me, do I?

Of course she didn't.

Of course I do!

Nate leaned even closer. *'Uh?'*

She tried to clear her head, but couldn't. Could only look at him now that the mistiness had left her glasses. 'Was that your question? To ask me to take my glasses off so you could see my——?'

'Big grey eyes?' He shifted the tiniest bit closer. Blurred the lines between *shelter* and *dangerous promise* a little more. That was the trouble with attractive, wolfish men. They could get a girl confused without even trying. 'I guess that depends.'

'Depends on what?' Despite all her reservations, despite resentment and suspicion and not being willing to trust his motives for being here for Henry right now, she leaned forward.

She wanted to feel the scratchiness of his day-old beard beneath her fingertips. Wanted to run her hands through his hair, and gauge the muscles hidden beneath that dangerous suit he wore.

Why did she want these things? This was Nate Barrett. She *shouldn't* want these things from him. All he had done was kiss her forehead, and the side of her mouth. She shouldn't have let him do that much. How could it leave her aching for more?

'I've always admired black,' she murmured. She wanted to run her hands over his midnight shirt, then wrap them around the strong column of his tanned, luscious-looking neck, bring his head down to hers, and...

It didn't help that he watched her with all the focused interest of one very predatorial male.

'You like black?' He raised an eyebrow. A *black* eyebrow. 'That's not my final question, by the way.'

'I meant I like the colour black. For clothing.' Did she even own any black clothes? 'I thought I might buy myself a, uh, a bowler hat. In, um, black.'

A bowler hat? In black. Oh, *groan*. 'You know. For fancy dress and stuff.'

His mouth twitched. She saw it. A little twitcheroonie,

right there at the left-hand corner. Despite herself, she liked that twitch.

She straightened, stepped back. Distanced herself as best as she physically could, and hoped her reactions would follow. 'We're wasting time. We should get to the office.'

'We're not finished, but I'll get us a taxi—'

'I have my car.' Good manners insisted she offer to drive him. Henry would expect it.

She led the way across the parking bays to the elderly yellow bug, praying he would forget all about whatever question he'd had in mind.

'Make yourself comfortable.' With her seat belt clipped, she sat bolt upright in her seat. It was as relaxed as she was likely to get with this man in her vicinity. 'It will take a couple of minutes for the engine to warm up enough for us to leave.'

She allowed the vehicle to idle, and looked anywhere other than at the man seated beside her. Awareness of his closeness, of the near-touching of their bodies, increased her nervousness. 'At least we'll get into the office nice and early. It's important to keep things running well for Henry.'

'Your commitment to my grandfather's health,' Nate drawled, 'and to the smooth-running of Montbank Shipping, is…commendable.'

While she pondered the hint of doubt in what should have been a clear-cut compliment, Nate punched a number into his cellphone.

Moments later, he had arranged for his grandfather's transfer to Acebrook private hospital. 'Praiseworthy indeed, if somewhat questionable in intent.'

'Yes,' she mumbled, her attention distracted by his ability to plan and organise Henry's transfer so seamlessly. This was clearly a man of action.

There's no need to dwell on the appeal of that trait. Five minutes ago his attitude struck you as overbearing and annoying. Besides, he might not always use such power for good.

Suddenly her thoughts caught up with what he had said, not just with the tone of his voice and its mesmerising quality.

Indignation narrowed her gaze as she turned to glare at him. 'Are you suggesting that my relationship with your grandfather is anything other than honest, respectful and completely appropriate on both sides?'

'*Is* the relationship appropriate on both sides?' His shrug was pure nonchalance. 'You appear to be hugely protective of him. I can't help but wonder what could possibly engender such a degree of commitment.'

'Then maybe you should contemplate the concepts of kindness and mutual respect,' she snapped, and crunched Gertrude's gearbox as she tried unsuccessfully to get the old car into first gear.

One minute the man made her want him and almost like him, and then this! Ooh, it made her blood boil.

Never drive while you're angry.

Bella's words of warning rang in her head. Chrissy dropped the car back into neutral, irritated that she had gone so close to being irresponsible simply because this man had annoyed her. He stirred her way too much.

A firm hand closed over hers where it rested on the gear stick.

'I see I was off base.' His deep words, although quiet, seemed to fill the small car space. 'I apologise.'

The warmth of that hand over hers was far too comforting and she thawed a little. But some of her anger remained. 'I care deeply about my boss. If that's a crime, then I'm guilty.'

'I'm glad…you've been here for him.' He squeezed her knuckles and let go.

Why hadn't *Nate* been here for Henry?

He's here now.
That's nowhere near enough.

'You'll make sure he doesn't feel as though things are out of his control, won't you, while you're running the company?'

She had intended to extract a promise. Instead, it came out as a plea, but she cared so much about Henry. He hadn't been himself lately, and now with the stroke—well, she just wanted him to have every chance to get better, that was all.

The scent of Nate's spicy aftershave came to her subtly as he turned to face her in the confines of the car. 'I'll respect his dignity as much as I can.'

'More zesty smells,' she muttered to herself. At least this one wouldn't tantalise her taste buds. 'We should leave now,' she snapped. 'The car's warm enough.'

And I'm even warmer!

She clamped her mouth tight as she eased Gertrude into the traffic and headed straight for the slowest-moving lane, where she wouldn't feel quite so bombarded by the volume of traffic.

'It's just that Henry hates to acknowledge that he's getting older.' She disliked the defensiveness in her tone. 'And there's no reason to think he won't be able to come back to work. It *was* a minor stroke.'

'Not so minor at his age and when he has other health considerations. Heart. Blood pressure…'

Henry would show him. Chrissy didn't know anyone with the amount of determination her boss had. Except maybe…his grandson.

Henry *would* be OK, wouldn't he? 'It was my fault,' she blurted. 'He wouldn't have had the stroke if I hadn't dragged him all over Melbourne that day.'

'Surely you don't believe that?' Nate's tone was openly

surprised. 'If a stroke is going to happen, it happens. And, in fact, the hospital staff told me your swift actions probably prevented an all-out heart attack.'

'Oh.' The load of guilt lifted somewhat. 'Well, what I did when the stroke happened was little enough.'

Her hands tightened on the wheel as she fought to suppress the memories of the frightening event. And acknowledged how ungracious she had been back in Henry's hospital room. 'I'm sorry I tried to discourage you from taking over Henry's work. I was out of line.'

'Perhaps we should both forget the way we started this morning, and begin afresh.' The suggestion was almost toneless. Definitely uninterested.

Just like that, he had turned off all feelings of attraction to her?

So much for thinking they had both been whapped in the face by it earlier. Whatever had happened, Nate Barrett had apparently simply *chosen* to be over it.

A humbling thought, but then, she wasn't anything special, was she? She certainly hadn't been special enough to hold her parents' interest.

That's over, and this is now, and has to be dealt with now. Her pride swelled to her rescue. 'I couldn't agree more. The only things that matter are those that relate to my boss's recovery.'

'I'm glad we've achieved Feng Shui on the matter.'

Was he being sarcastic? Somehow she couldn't see this man putting himself out to try to live in harmony with the natural elements and forces of the earth. He would be more likely to try to bend them to *his* natural force!

'Uh, right, then.' She accidentally tramped the brakes a bit too hard when a car in front of her slowed suddenly, but he simply sat there, apparently calm.

Bella always ground her teeth. She thought Chrissy couldn't hear it, but she could.

Once she was comfortable in the flow of traffic again, Nate spoke. 'I see you're on your provisional plates. How long have you been driving?'

'I spent *mumble mumble* years on my learner's licence. I got my provisional one a month ago.' It wasn't that driving scared her, exactly. She just found it uncomfortable. 'I don't drive as smoothly as I'd like to yet, but Gertrude has been very forgiving when I've crunched her gears and things like that.'

'Gertrude, huh?'

'Well, Gertie for short, but yes. It suits her, don't you think?' What else could three sisters name a bright yellow, elderly bug they all adored, other than Gertrude?

When she finally parked, after three tries, almost neatly in an allotted space beneath the Montbank office building, she sighed with relief. Nothing was outside the lines, anyway.

Nate offered a smile. 'You did very well. It's better to be a bit careful until you gain more experience.'

After a moment—once she'd got over the impact of that smile and his encouraging words—she realised she was smiling back. 'Thank you.'

Maybe having him here wouldn't be so awful. Maybe his presence would actually lighten the load while Henry got better.

If she could just overcome her attraction to him.

CHAPTER THREE

WHILE Chrissy gathered her travel mug, notebook, large shoulder bag and the canvas holdall that held the latest potted plants she had rescued from the last-ditch discount table at the supermarket, Nate exited the car. His gaze lingered on the bag of plants, his expression quizzical.

So she tried to save lost plants. Was that a crime? Defensiveness made her sharp. 'Is something wrong?'

'Not at all.' He glanced from her to the paraphernalia and back, almost smiled, then shook his head. 'Would you like some help?'

'I can manage.' She locked her car door. 'I always have this much stuff with me.' Which made her sound like a packhorse.

'Just give me the holdall, then.' He stretched out his hand, clearly expecting her to yield up some of her bounty for him to carry.

Admit it. You'd like to yield in other ways.

Bah! She really could do without these conflicting feelings. Yet he had such a nice hand. Lean, with long, straight fingers. The same fingers that had stroked her face earlier. That had covered her hand so comfortingly. Not that she was fixated about his hands or anything.

'Chrissy? The holdall?' he prompted.

'Oh, fine. If you insist on helping, here you go.' She allowed him to take the bag from her. After all, she had nothing to prove.

He offered a wry smile as he took the bag. 'Thank you.'

When their hands touched, that zing happened again. It made her imagine all sorts of hand-related things she shouldn't. Heat swarmed up her chest and into her face, because she had just proved something she really didn't want to prove.

Ergo, that she hadn't been able to distance herself from this very sensual man one iota.

'Something tells me it's going to be a very long day.' She made the pronouncement as they travelled into the building via the key-coded lift. Travel by stairs would have been preferable, but those were inaccessible from outside the building.

Their reflections stared back solemnly from the steel-plated doors. She and Nate Barrett, side by side and looking far too right that way for her comfort. 'I mean, the day will be busy and demanding.'

'I imagine it will.' His gaze skimmed the coil of hair on top of her head, moved to her mouth and returned to her eyes. She saw it all in the reflection of polished doors. Yet it felt as though he had touched her. Caressed her.

'What's on the agenda today?' He barked it out. 'Any big problems looming?'

Any big problems? How about the problem of this unwanted attraction? She had thought he no longer felt it, but now realised he still did.

'There are several things that will need attention today.' Not one specific matter would surface in her brain. 'I'll be happy to debrief you when we get upstairs.' Her face heated again. 'I mean, I'll *brief* you. I mean—'

'I get the picture.'

At the roughness of his tone, a part of her rejoiced. She told herself that was simply because she saw no reason why she should suffer the attraction alone.

When the lift eased to a stop she stepped out gratefully. Perhaps the distraction of work would overrule the responses he drew from her. 'Here we are. The hub of Montbank Shipping. As you worked here before you made your move overseas, I guess it'll be quite familiar to you.'

Despite all the years you've stayed away.

She would remember to keep him in the place of the deserting grandson yet. At the thought she sobered, because in truth he *was* that person, and she could never reconcile herself to that. No matter how much he made her want him, or how much she thought he might want her.

One abandonment in her lifetime was enough.

Nate nodded to several ancillary staff who obviously knew him. They all showed their shock at seeing him. He seemed a little unsettled, too.

'How does it feel to come back after so long? Does it make you melancholy?'

'There *is* a world outside these doors, you know.' His retort labelled her as unadventurous and insular.

Chrissy gritted her teeth.

When they were alone again, he asked, with a hint of disbelief, 'Are you the only new staff member since I left? I knew the firm was close-knit, but—'

'On this floor, I am, yes.' So what if they liked to build an atmosphere of family among the employees?

She had been welcomed when she'd started here. He had no idea how much she had needed that. 'I got the job as Henry's PA straight out of school when his previous PA retired to the Gold Coast. All the company members were sad to see her go.'

Unlike the PA, Nate had returned, albeit only for the

duration of Henry's recovery. She hoped people would understand the temporary nature of his visit.

On that surprisingly depressing thought, she flung open the door to Henry's suite of offices and stepped inside. 'I'll just be one minute.'

This was her territory. Among her ceiling chimes and experimental wall art and, of course, potted plants, she felt secure. At home. In charge.

After quickly disposing of the killed-off plants in the corner stand—it was always a bit sad—she replaced them with the new ones. From now, she had only one choice. She must think business and nothing but business for the duration of Nate Barrett's stay.

Given the mixed emotions he brought out in her, it was the only hope she had of holding on to her sanity. 'The UK imports first, I think.'

'By all means.' His agreement smacked of condescension. She ignored it and launched into a list of problematical import issues.

He was swift to pick things up. He had a sharp mind and a decisive attitude, and he knew the business.

'There's also this lot of stuff.' She brought in a pile of files.

They worked almost seamlessly then broke for lunch. Aside from the odd distraction, such as when she noticed he had a tiny birthmark high on his forehead and wanted to trace it with a fingertip, she managed to remain acceptably aloof.

It was early afternoon by the time they had cleared through the bulk of the most urgent work.

He sat back in his chair and rolled his shoulders. 'Now that the worst is taken care of, I want a meeting with all the department heads. I need to let them know about Henry's stroke, and get a verbal status on each of their areas.

'Hopefully one of them will fit...' He turned his head to

glance out the window at the fog-shrouded cityscape. 'You mentioned a difficulty with the stevedore company?'

'They're usually very good, so I don't know what the problem can be, but yes, a memo came through earlier.' She gathered their used coffee mugs and headed toward the kitchenette just off their offices.

Instead of remaining at his desk, Nate rose and followed. Immediately her awareness of him cranked up, and she had been doing so well, too.

You mean you'd managed to live in denial for a few moments.

'I'll phone the company right after I organise the meeting with the department heads.'

'No need.' He prowled behind her. 'I'll speak to the stevedore people while you arrange the meeting.'

She considered protesting, then changed her mind. Why waste her breath? If he wanted to micromanage the matter, let him. 'As you wish.'

'That's settled, then.' But he kept pace behind her, and she remained deeply aware of him the whole time.

'How old are you?' he asked abruptly. 'Twenty-four?'

'Yes. How old are *you*?' She looked over her shoulder at him. Her words had a hint of goading that she couldn't quite control. 'Thirty-five? Thirty-eight? Forty, maybe?'

'I'll be thirty in December.'

'My condolences,' she quipped, but the spark in his eyes undermined her efforts to keep her interest in him at bay.

She stopped in front of the sink with her back turned to him, and simply didn't know what to do. His awareness of her was palpable, and she responded to that awareness on a deep, instinctual level.

Her life plan didn't include involvements with men who dodged commitment. No matter how much those men might—incomprehensibly—attract her.

She remained still and silent, and hoped he would ease back. Give her the breathing space she needed. She did *not* want him to move closer and answer her earlier question of how it would feel if he closed the distance between them completely.

Instead of moving away, he made a soft sound of frustration and shifted closer. 'What is it about you? I can't be in the same room as you without—'

'It's nothing. Nothing at all.' She spun around, aggravation, curiosity and awareness bursting out at her seams. She had to get away before she did something stupid. Like welcome his closeness.

He shook his head. 'You don't believe that.'

'I have to.' Instead of getting clear of him, in her haste she smacked straight into him.

They both gasped. His hands encircled her upper arms. His deep blue eyes stared into her grey ones. Desire burned for her in that gaze.

All right. She admitted it. She wanted him to kiss her until they both stopped breathing. So there. It didn't mean they should actually do it.

As though sensing her confusion, he stepped forward. Feet braced apart, he brought her into the cradle of his body.

She should have resisted, but couldn't. Could only speak words to try to negate her body's betrayal. 'I don't want this. We don't even know each other.'

'Don't we? I *feel* as though I know you.' His confusion rang in his voice. 'You're so familiar to me that it seems I've always known you.'

His words echoed the feeling deep inside her.

He inhaled deeply against her hair and sighed. 'Your hair drives me mad. I want to unwind it. Let it fall, and see how long it is. I want to tug out those damned chopsticks and—'

She finally found words. Resistance. 'We shouldn't be doing this.' Her breath caught in a sexy little sound in the back of her throat. Hoping he hadn't heard it, she pushed free of his hold. 'We're just two people brought together by a common goal. To get Henry better.'

'I agree, but I think we both know there's more at work here than that. I don't understand it, really. In general I don't go for women who…' He waved a hand, apparently unable to articulate just how incomprehensible he found his attraction to her.

Well, thanks for nothing, Mr Nate Barrett! 'It's all right,' she assured him with more than a hint of antagonism in her tone. 'I find you repulsive on a personal level, too.'

'I guess I asked for that. I'm afraid being around you—wanting you—appears to affect my communication skills.' After a long moment spent searching her expression, he seemed to come to a conclusion.

'Something about me, or about being attracted to me, scares you. What is it?' Although the question was asked in a silken tone, it scraped over her like gravel shifting in a dry, abandoned streambed. Because it was way too close to the truth for comfort.

'You don't scare me. Why would you? You're just here to fill in while Henry gets better.' She tried to inject strength into her tone. 'I can assure you—'

'Something has you determined to keep me at a distance.' He pushed one hand through his thick hair, ruffling it. 'If not fear, then what, exactly? We're attracted to each other. You clearly don't want a deep involvement with me. I don't want that, either, but we could enjoy the moment. What would it hurt?'

'I'm not into casual liaisons with virtual strangers.' His words had stung her, but she should have *known*. Should have expected exactly this from a man who had deserted his grandfather without the slightest hesitation.

His glance roved over her again—assessing, thoughtful. He spoke without acknowledging her words. 'Or is it all men that you want to keep at bay?'

'Just because I haven't had any serious relationships...' She would be able to commit if the circumstances were right. 'If you must know, I simply haven't met the appropriate man yet. When I do I'll know it, and I won't hesitate to put myself at his mercy.'

'Well, well.' His eyebrows lifted.

She wanted to knock that *I know what's going on inside your poor misguided psyche* look right off his face.

The man was delving into her deepest secrets. Pulling them out to the harsh light of examination. He had no right to do that. Nor to expect her to fall into his arms for the day or week or two that he would be here.

Her temper flared and words poured out. 'You don't scare me, Nate. I simply don't particularly like you.

'You abandoned your grandfather for over six years. It took a stroke for you to return. What do you expect me to say? I'm not interested in the kind of relationship you just insulted me by offering.'

The more she said, the more her hurt and anger burned and the more words came out. 'I don't want *any* kind of relationship with you, outside the minimum needed for us to function together in the office while you're here.

'In fairness, I'm sure I'm not the kind of woman you could possibly want, either. I think it's best if we forget all of this. Now, please excuse me. The business meeting needs to be organised.'

CHAPTER FOUR

'AT LEAST Margaret has given it a rest today.' Nate hit the appropriate key to shut off his computer with more force than finesse.

The screen went black, and he got to his feet, retrieved his suit jacket and shrugged into it. His outdoor coat followed. Five days had never been more of a trial. *Nor more stimulating*, a voice in his brain added, much to his disgust.

Hell, not because of Margaret. The woman was a pariah. He hoped he had finally convinced her to stop phoning the office and sending him emails in her pathetic, transparent attempts to rekindle something between them that had never existed in the first place.

Her barely veiled efforts to find out about the financial affairs of the company he brushed off utterly.

His firm of lawyers had made it clear that she would get nowhere if she tried again to have Henry declared unfit, or to get financial control of anything outside of her allowance. She simply needed to accept defeat.

'Thank you, Mr Dimitri. Mr Barrett may not have time to attend, but I'll bring your advertising affair to his attention.' The sound of Chrissy's voice as she wound up a call in the next room stirred Nate's senses.

He heard her moving about the room, no doubt gathering the truckload of things she ferried to and from the office daily.

That use of the word *affair* brought instant recall of his heated words with her at the start of the week when he'd tried to make her see they could be good together.

'Are you about finished in there?' He rapped out the question as he snatched up his briefcase. 'I can't lock the strongroom until I know you're done.'

And locking the strongroom and getting out of here is something I really want to do, because I've had about enough of trying to make sense of the discrepancies in the accounting that I discovered earlier today!

Nate hadn't had time to discuss the matter with her. Wasn't sure he would until he'd worked out the problem.

Getting away doesn't work when you go home to Henry's hideaway cottage each night. You think of her, anyway.

At least the cottage was one place Margaret wouldn't find him. For some reason, Henry had never told Margaret of the small home, although Chrissy knew of its existence.

'I'm noting a call.' Chrissy's arctic tone managed to convey both superiority and disapproval. 'Forgive me if I take my job seriously!'

'Fine. Whatever.' He didn't want to reminisce about the cottage. He just wanted to take her there and ravish her for as long as it suited him.

For the first time in his life he wanted a woman who was completely unsuited to him, and he couldn't seem to stop the attraction.

Out of control was not a place Nate liked to be. He stalked into her office. 'Who's this Dimitri person, and what did he want?' He stopped so abruptly that the tails of his coat flapped against the backs of his legs.

Chrissy had just stuffed a sheaf of papers into her holdall-style shoulder bag. Face flushed, gaze sliding anywhere but his way, she looked guilty as hell.

She might take a lot of things to and from the office, but they were personal items.

His mind leaped ahead. Supplied him with an answer to a question he hadn't fully formulated yet. A sick feeling of disbelief started up in his stomach.

Tell me there's some simple explanation, Chrissy, because I really don't want to believe the worst of you.

The head of the stevedore company had phoned him again today. His concerns over last-minute alterations to shipping lists had been strong enough for Nate to instigate a discreet investigation of matters at the docks. He had suspected lax business practices on someone's part. If it was more than that, if Chrissy was somehow involved...

'Perhaps you might like to tell me what you just put in your bag.' His tone was harsh, his expression no doubt as tight as it felt, but what could he do except demand an explanation?

She fussed with the bag, then slung it over her shoulder with a defiant flip of her hand. 'It's nothing. Just a few things I need to take home.'

'The papers looked like computer printouts.' He took a step toward her. 'Why would you need to take your work home? You haven't mentioned anything about it to me.'

Give me an explanation, Chrissy. Help me out here.

'Well, I didn't know you had bionic vision to see so much in one short glimpse.' Sarcasm. A sweep of her desk with her gaze. She turned toward the door. 'If I don't cross paths with you at Henry's hospital, I guess I'll see you Monday.'

Dismissed. Just like that. Even though *he* was the one with the questions. The one who needed her to reassure him she had nothing to hide.

With a flounce and a sway of her bottom—covered in a red velvet skirt today, thank you very much—she strolled out the door. That bottom sway had been deliberate. He was convinced of it. Still, she was certainly cool under fire if she *was* hiding something from him.

'You can't get away from me that easily.' He locked the strongroom, stalked out of the office and followed her into the corridor.

'I'm not trying to *get away*.' She cast a disgruntled look his way and kept walking, buttoning her burgundy coat with one hand as she moved. 'I'm simply going home for the night. That is allowed, you know.'

He wanted her to be innocent of any wrongdoing. It was a demand somewhere deep inside him. From a place that wanted to believe in her, even though he shouldn't care one way or the other.

It must be the knowledge that she cared so much for his grandfather. Nate's own guilt at leaving Henry alone so much in past years ate at him.

Henry wanted him to stay. Permanently. It was in his eyes each time Nate visited him at the hospital. Nate couldn't do that, and maybe he had comforted himself with the knowledge that Chrissy had been there for his grandfather. That she would go on being there for Henry.

How much did she really care, though, if she was hiding secrets? *She can't be hiding secrets. You must have it wrong somehow.* 'Why won't you tell me—?'

'There's nothing to tell.' She all but snapped the words, but that flush was there again on her face. 'I'm only trying to help Henry.'

'Then tell me what's in your bag.' He was a few steps behind her when she almost collided with Margaret Montbank as the woman emerged from the deserted tracking-department offices.

Aggravation coiled inside him. 'What are you doing here, Margaret?'

Margaret's initial shock gave way to arrogant bluster. 'My husband owns this company. Why shouldn't I be here? But, as it happens, I'm just leaving. Goodnight.' She turned her back with the clear intention of suiting action to words.

Now Nate had *two* women trying to block his knowledge of what they were up to. His aggravation levels expanded accordingly. He stepped toward Margaret. 'Wait a moment, please.'

Chrissy stepped forward, too. 'Do tell us, Mrs Montbank. What brings you here?'

Nate hadn't expected Chrissy to intervene. He should have realised she would.

Margaret's polite mask slipped, revealing frustration and resentment. 'Don't question me in that tone, you snide little—'

'That's enough.' It took Nate a moment to realise he had placed himself between his grandfather's PA and Margaret in case the need to protect Chrissy arose.

Somewhat archaic of him. And Chrissy was probably the last person on earth who would need, or welcome, such a surge of protectiveness.

In a sudden change of tactic, Margaret tossed back her shoulder-length swathe of bottle-blonde hair and preened at him. 'You're so edgy, Nate. Couldn't I have simply come here tonight to see you, darling?'

'Bleurgh.' Chrissy attempted, unsuccessfully, to turn her sound of disgust into a cough.

Surprisingly, much of Nate's aggravation slid away in response to that small, sarcastic sound.

Henry's wife offered a saccharine smile. 'Oh, that's right. The little secretary believes she has you all to herself, doesn't she?'

Nate knew instantly where Margaret intended to take this. '*Margaret.*'

'Don't worry, Nate, dear.' She lifted one arm, revealing a diamond-studded bracelet that had no doubt cost his grandfather a bomb. 'I won't tell Chrissy about our little affair six years ago. You were just a boy, really, not long out of university, and so smitten with me, the slightly older woman.'

'Slightly older?' He suppressed the ridiculing guffaw, but couldn't stop the fury that was unleashed inside him. What gave her the right to put into words her own blatantly unfaithful attitude that had driven him away six years ago? He had left to save Henry from learning of it.

Yet she casually brought the subject up as though she didn't give a damn who knew what she had tried to do.

'This had better be the first time you've referred to that. And you damned well know there was no—'

'Please tell me what you wanted in the tracking department, Mrs Montbank.' Chrissy's tone was pure office bland. The steam radiating from her was another thing altogether. She had clearly taken Margaret's story and swallowed it whole.

Says a lot for what she thinks of you, Barrett.

Unaware of his thoughts, Chrissy addressed Margaret again. 'It's after hours now, as I'm sure you realised when you discovered the department was closed for the night, but I'd be happy to take a message for one of the tracking staff for Monday.'

'I simply wanted to say hello to Janice Deanne. She should have been working late. I didn't believe…' She stopped abruptly.

Nate's eyes narrowed. 'Stay away from the company, Margaret. I won't warn you again.'

Farther down the corridor, a senior staff member exited an office and wearily rubbed his eyes. Nate motioned the man over. 'Would you see Mrs Montbank to her vehicle? She's finished here and won't be back.'

'Certainly.' The man gave Margaret a cool glance, and led her toward the lifts. 'I'll be happy to see you off the premises, Mrs Montbank.'

'I only dropped in.' Margaret glared at the man, then at Nate. 'It was an idle visit, nothing more.'

'Whatever you say, Mrs Montbank.' The man clearly thought about as much of her as Nate did.

Nate grinned as the pair stepped into the lift and disappeared.

His grin faded when Chrissy turned on him, her expression fierce.

'You had an affair with Margaret.' Her voice shook. The disgust and accusation in her words filled the air. 'She hinted at it the day I met you, but I didn't want to believe it. She was Henry's wife. Did he know?

'Is that why you left so suddenly? Because he found out and banished you? It's a wonder he even allows you a salary in the business, after what you've done to him.'

'Actually, I own…' He stopped abruptly. If Henry hadn't told her of the situation, then she wouldn't hear it from him. Besides, he didn't want the knowledge of his wealth involved in this.

Even in anger, he wanted Chrissy's reactions to be for him, not for his balance sheets. 'You sure know how to jump to conclusions, don't you? There was nothing between Margaret and me, not ever, and my reasons for leaving are none of your business.'

'I don't believe you.' The mutinous sparkle of her eyes behind her glasses confirmed her statement. 'Why would Margaret say such a thing if it weren't true?'

'Because she's full of her own self-importance, doesn't care about the feelings of those around her, and because she's a troublemaker.' *Because she has somehow discerned the depth of attraction you hold for me, and she resents it.*

She wavered, then lifted her chin. 'Look me in the eye and deny there was anything between you.'

He saw it then. The jealousy behind the fury. In response he wanted to back her up against the wall and kiss her to oblivion. 'Why do you care so much?'

'I care because of *Henry*.'

'My grandfather isn't the only reason.' He knew it as clearly as she did, and he was ready to deal with this. Forget trying to ignore it any longer.

Fighting still, she turned and stalked toward the lifts. 'You egotistical…*man*.'

He followed. 'Do you really think I could want that woman? Come on, Chrissy.'

Margaret was the antithesis of the woman before him. Shallow where Chrissy was deep and caring. Harsh where Chrissy was kind and soft.

He hadn't realised until this moment that his attraction to Chrissy had reached beyond the purely physical, to delve into the personality beneath. It was a troubling knowledge, but not enough to stop him. Not now.

The empty lift slid open. She hesitated outside it. That slight hesitation was enough to make him cover the distance between them. To clasp her shoulders and look deep into her eyes when he asked it again. 'Do you believe that of me, Chrissy? Tell me.'

'I want to, but no.' She seemed to fight her own frustration. 'I can't believe it. Not really.'

'Because you know I want *you*. For my sins.' And *she* wanted *him*. These facts were utterly clear to him. Maybe not as much to her.

He could show her. Could explain it with something more powerful than words. He *wanted* to show her. 'Because of this.'

If she had pushed away, or indicated in any way that she

didn't want this as much as he did, he would have stopped. Instead, the culmination of a week's hunger and refutation revealed itself in their kiss, in the way their bodies pressed to each other, homing in on all that had been denied between them.

She tasted of everything he had ever wanted and never had. Her mouth melted under his, welcoming him even as her body arched closer. He cupped her jaw, his fingers splaying down over the soft skin of her neck.

'So soft.' His other hand pressed against her shoulders, feeling delicate bone beneath the layers of clothing. He wanted to strip it all away and just feel Chrissy. The words breathed out against her mouth. 'I want you. I've wanted this since the moment we met.'

A kiss to slake his hunger. To prove that kissing her wasn't such a thing to long for. He almost laughed, because now that he had kissed her, he simply wanted more. More and more of Chrissy Gable, in every way he could have her. Whatever she would give.

'Kiss me again, Christianna.' He bent his head once more and acknowledged the need. For fulfilment in her, yes. Definitely that. But for other things, too. Undefined things that even now threatened him in ways he couldn't comprehend.

'Nate.' Just his name, breathed out on the same kind of sexy little sigh that had tortured him once before.

He caught her open mouth and plundered deep, and she met him, tangled her tongue with his with frank enthusiasm. Her response made him crazy. Rushed his blood to every flashpoint.

His hands curved, just once, around the soft flesh of her bottom. Shaped her while his imagination went wild. While he pictured them together at his grandfather's cottage, making love night after night.

Except Nate didn't do *night after night* with all it entailed. It was too easy to forget it in her arms. He fought for sanity. Fought to keep from losing himself. From freefalling into something that came as close to scaring him as anything could.

Instead, he grated words from a throat roughened with desire. 'Tell me…what's in your bag.'

'Tell me why you went away.' Her words were breathless, kiss-clogged, but as aggressive as she could make them.

'I can't do that.' For the first time, he wished he could talk about it. Regretted the secret. Despite her anger, his fingers caressed her arms, ached even now to touch her bare skin. 'What were those sheets of paper?'

'You keep your secrets, but I can't have mine?' She wrenched free.

He didn't try to touch her again, although he wanted to. Wanted to hold her close while he showed her again how volatile she made him feel.

'I'm working on something that meant a lot to Henry, if you must know.' At another time, her haughty anger would have made him smile. 'And since it's *his* project, and nothing to do with work, I don't see why I should explain it to you.'

Nate saw, though. Remembered belatedly just why he needed her answer. He would get it in the end. 'It's late. Let me see you home.'

'There's no need. Gertie—'

'Didn't accompany you to work today.' He knew, because Chrissy had arrived at work before him this morning. He would have seen the car in the car park, had she driven it. He noticed far too much about her.

'Well, that's right, actually.' She floundered, and her pale face flushed again. 'I forgot for a minute that I didn't have the car.' The admission was grudging. 'But that's fine, because I'll just take public transport. I really don't need a lift.'

'It's no big deal.' He pushed the button on the elevator. When it opened again, he took her elbow and guided her inside.

His hand remained as the doors closed. He liked to believe it was choice that kept it there. 'I'd like to meet your sisters, anyway. That is, if you expect either of them to be at your flat tonight? I understand they both know my grandfather reasonably well.'

This was the weekend, though. Parties. Dates. Clubs and pubs and lots of men on the prowl. The thought of Chrissy out on a date with any one of them made him grit his teeth.

'Regardless of whether your sisters are there or not, I'm taking you home.' Something primitive and possessive welled inside him. 'So don't argue.'

CHAPTER FIVE

'YOU could do with being a little less bossy sometimes, but I'll accept the ride, I guess, since you're so insistent about it.' Chrissy cast an unsteady glance in Nate's direction. 'As for your question, we live in half a terraced house.'

Who wanted to talk about anything when their senses still swirled from such a kiss? Oh, my, that kiss! Her body blazed from what Nate had brought to life in those moments in the hallway. His kiss had been so much more than just a physical mating of mouths.

You heard him question you about what was in your bag straight after. For all you know he might have staged the kiss to catch you off guard so he could get his answer.

It didn't matter what had motivated him. Well, of course it *mattered*, but the kiss itself had affected him as much as it had her.

'Half a terraced house exactly where?' His question was innocuous enough. But he had a tight, leashed look about him that gave her a delicious shiver. The sort of look that warned, *Just do one thing to provoke me and it'll start all over again.*

'Um…' She wanted to crow about that look. Wanted to do just one thing and see what happened. These weren't the right reactions.

So he's not the type to hang around. Why not do what he suggested on Monday, and take him up on the short-term liaison he had in mind?

Chrissy was actually tempted, which shocked her to the soles of her never-get-involved-with-a-noncommittal-man shoes.

'Ah, the address is, ah…' She gave him the details in a breathy voice she didn't want to admit was her own. And yes. She expected her sisters to be there tonight. They had all planned very carefully to ensure that would be the case, but introduce Nate to them…?

Not if she could help it. The jealous, possessive thought made her gasp. Bella and Soph were beauties, while Chrissy was…just Chrissy. But she accepted that. She had never wanted to keep a man away from them before.

That's because you've never cared about losing one to them before.

Deep down, she had to admit that was true. Her sisters had never tried to steal anyone's attention from her, but it would happen anyway. Even their erstwhile parents, not exactly the best examples of commitment, had preferred Soph and Bella over Chrissy. Until Chrissy drove them to leave all three of their offspring.

She stifled a sigh and tucked the guilt back into its corner, where she could live with it in relative peace.

And talked on about her home, because she didn't want a thickening silence with all sorts of possibilities floating around in it to tempt her. 'We rent the upper floor. Our landlady is…batty, but nice. We're really lucky to have the place.'

'Dodging the issue, Chrissy?' With those few words, he nailed her procrastination to the wall.

When he strode out of the lift, she had to trot to keep up. 'I'm not dodging anything. I was simply discussing my home. Sorry if you weren't interested!'

The sound he made had a definite sensual edge to it. 'I think you can take it as a given that I'm interested.'

'Oh, um, well.' For a man who was interested, he moved as though he couldn't get away fast enough. 'Could you slow down a bit? My feet are about to fall off.'

He slowed, took her hand and tucked it through his arm, effectively clamping her to his warm, hard side. 'Just match your steps to mine now and don't try to fight it.'

Don't try to fight it?

Her feelings were already on the rampage, and that was his best advice?

Feelings? I am not emotionally involved with this man. It's a simple case of physical attraction. Y chromosome meets non-Y chromosome, and they just sort of, well…attract.

Even to her, the reasoning sounded weak. 'Why are you so keen to meet Bella and Soph? For that matter, how do you know all this stuff about me?'

'I *have* phoned my grandfather from time to time in the past six years, you know. Sometimes he talked about you.'

His bored tone couldn't have made it plainer that he might want to kiss her, might find her physically attractive, but, as a person, she left him cold.

'Good.' She tightened her fingers on his arm and smiled through teeth that no longer wanted quite so much to nibble on his earlobe as to chomp a hole through it. 'I hope he told you all about me.'

In the most boring fashion imaginable, right down to my fetish for toe socks with cartoon characters on them, and the fact that I can't put those stupid ring-binders back together after I've opened them to add new plastic sheets.

Nate's mouth twitcherooed. For the second time.

And Chrissy seethed. How dared he find her amusing when he had just insulted her?

Then he glanced at her and his smile faded, replaced by a sort of determined resignation that she didn't understand. 'Why don't we drive out to the hospital before I take you home? We can say hello to Henry and report in about work, if he's interested.'

Checkmated. That easily. She couldn't refuse the chance to see Henry.

'That's a lot of trouble for you.' He caught her out like that from time to time—being thoughtful and considerate—and it unnerved her.

As had happened yesterday when he insisted on knowing what Henry's comment about Thursday lattes had been about, then took her out for her favourite coffee blend when she explained the weekly tradition to him. Aside from an underlying awareness of him that reared up from time to time, she had almost enjoyed that outing.

Admit it. The man can be a charming companion.

'It's no trouble, but why don't you have your car today?'

She felt his stomach muscles move against her hand as he walked. It was just too distracting. 'I…ah.'

'Is there something wrong with it?'

'Wrong with…' Oh, right. With the car. 'No. Gertie's fine. Our mechanic looks after her.'

Joe was also their friend and neighbour and ran a successful suburban auto-shop, although he did a lot of the work on their car for free. He had even helped out with driving lessons for Chrissy and Soph. Bella had already been driving when they met him.

In return for Joe's help, Soph styled his hair, Bella introduced him to men she thought he might find interesting and Chrissy occasionally blitzed his work office so he could find his desk again. It was an arrangement that suited all of them.

'It's just that it was really Soph's week to have the car.

Bella was last week. I'm supposed to be next week, but I'll give most of it back to Soph. We mix and match to suit our schedules.'

'Right.' He probably had no idea what she was nattering on about.

Who could blame him? She should simply make the smart decision and back right away from him. So why didn't she? She couldn't *really* be contemplating throwing her hat over the short-term-affair-windmill, so to speak?

Getting involved with him would be insanity. Think about that instead of hats and windmills. Think of how you'd feel when he left!

When he led her to a retro convertible in the car park, she had to hold back a gasp. Long, sleek lines. Bright red paintwork. Cream top. Gorgeous leather interior. It was a shamelessly sexy car that pushed thoughts of restraint and caution from her head.

Indeed, this car roused some very sensual thoughts. What a great match for…Gertie. Yes. A smooth, powerful car that would set off the bug's quaintness to perfection. Their cars should be parked side by side, to show them to advantage. Simply for the aesthetics of it. No other reason.

Chrissy suppressed a growl, disgusted with herself. No other reason, indeed. Next thing she would have the cars sharing a twin garage beside a cosy little house somewhere in the suburbs.

'Suburbs, affairs,' she muttered. 'You wouldn't know what you wanted if it came right up and bit you on *That Feature That Shall Not Be Named.*'

Nate seemed content to drive to the hospital in silence. Maybe because he thought he was travelling with a deranged lunatic who muttered to herself all the time!

The quiet should have given her time to pull herself together. Might have, if she hadn't been overwhelmed by the sweet rumble of the car's engine. By the plush welcome of its wide bench seat that carried a faint scent of…Nate.

Why did his car have to communicate the very essence of him? She felt as though the whole dratted vehicle was an extension of being held in his arms.

It was a relief to focus on Henry when they arrived. Until she realised that, although he was in better health, her boss was in poorer spirits. He did his best to sound cheerful, but she saw through it, and worried.

After a short discussion of a general nature, Henry started to fiddle with the bedcovers. He seemed almost furtive, which didn't make sense. 'Don't work too hard, Nate. Just take care of the day-to-day things.'

He eased back against his pillows, his face pinched. 'Leave the monthly tasks and so forth. I'll be ready to take care of those more mundane things soon, anyway.'

'I'm getting by.' Nate said it gently, but Chrissy knew from working with him that he would never *just get by*. The man applied himself wholly to whatever he worked on. As he had proved when he kissed her.

No more kissy thoughts already!

They didn't visit for long after that. Nate said he would return tomorrow. Chrissy noted the time and decided that her visit could wait until later in the day. Not that she felt driven to avoid Nate just because she couldn't get his kiss out of her mind.

Oh, so fine, then. She really needed some distance so she could pull her head together! It was all Nate's fault, anyway. He wasn't turning out to be the simple, uncomplicated rat she had first thought him to be.

She settled into her seat in his car and clipped her seat belt with aggravated vigour.

'He's a far more complex rat,' she muttered. A nice rat,

with depths and layers she wanted to explore despite the clear likelihood of getting herself well and truly burnt as a result of her curiosity.

'Were you talking to me?' An eyebrows lifted.

Oh, good. He has bionic hearing as well as bionic eyesight. Did that mean he had understood her earlier mumbled comment, about the car and the suburbs and—just exactly what had she said?

'Are the doctors happy with Henry's progress?' Her glare dared him to say anything about her muttering, now or earlier. After all, she hadn't seriously considered throwing herself at his feet dressed only in a bright red bow and a smile and asking him to sweep her away for a few nights and days of grand passion.

Her grump factor notched upward. 'What feedback have you had?'

'They're pleased with his recovery.' He looked at her thoughtfully. 'His speech has improved substantially and he's no longer disoriented.'

All this aligned with her own impressions, and focusing on Henry was a good idea right now. It had to beat thinking about Nate and red ribbons. 'But?'

'Emotionally he doesn't seem to be recovering as well as could be hoped. I would have thought you would take care of monthly reports and so forth, by the way.'

'I do some of them, but there are others that Henry has taken over in the past year or so. I'll be happy to do them again, but I'd rather Henry didn't know. I don't want him to think I'm stepping over the boundaries.'

'Fair enough. They're a few weeks off yet, anyway.' Nate turned the car back toward the city and lapsed again into silence.

He didn't seem to want to pull the car off the road and test out the manoeuvrability of its bench seating.

Chrissy shouldn't be thinking about that, either. Her focus should be solely on the care of her boss. 'I wish we could do more.'

She could be supportive, though. Tonight's project would be a good start. With a sigh, she relaxed against the leather seat. 'I'll be glad to get home.'

'Can't wait to be out of my company?'

Just when she thought they had left all that behind, Nate brought it up again. Drat the man.

'It's not intended as an offence to you.' Avoiding him was the wisest course. It didn't mean she anticipated the idea with any pleasure.

She ran a hand over the dashboard. When she spoke again, it was to address something completely different. 'Your choice of car surprises me.'

Are you as romantic as this car suggests?

He certainly wasn't. The man might own a made-for-romance car, but he had a run-from-commitment outlook.

'I rebuilt the car years ago. When I left Australia, Henry took over the registration. He's had a mechanic looking after it, driving it occasionally to keep it in shape.' Bland. Factual. *Not romantic.*

'Oh. I see.' Aspirations firmly squelched, she lapsed into silence and told herself to be glad he had reminded her of his true nature.

Inexplicably, she almost drifted off to sleep. She became fully alert in a hurry again when he found a parking place a few doors down from her home and climbed out of the car.

This was brush-Nate-off time. She should have been awake and prepared, not half-asleep with her head lolling in his direction.

'Thank you for taking me to see Henry, and for bringing me home.' Polite while firmly pushing him off. That was the way to manage this. Then she could go inside and collapse in private.

Or, at least, in as much privacy as a girl ever got when she shared an apartment with her sisters.

So brush him off now.

She didn't jingle her keys or fiddle with her shoulder bag. No subliminal I'd-like-to-invite-you-in signals were sent. She didn't *want* to invite him in. That would be stupid, now that she had remembered all the reasons they wouldn't suit each other.

Yet Chrissy's fingers itched. Positively itched. 'That's not because I want to jingle my keys. It's because I've been neglecting my hand-cream applications. Dry skin. It's nothing but dry skin.'

Nate pursed his mouth. A confused frown drew his brows down. 'Pardon?'

'Ah, nothing. Just thinking about an upcoming beauty treatment.' By the time she'd got the explanation out, Nate had her halfway up the external stairwell that led to her home. 'Well, thank you again for this. You must be in a hurry to—'

'Open the door for you.' He held out his hand for the key. 'Not in a hurry, but, nevertheless, we should go in. It's not exactly warm out here.'

Before she could A) hand her key over like a robotic ninny, or B) blurt out some brainless rejoinder like a robotic ninny, the door flew open from the inside.

Two gloriously beautiful women, one in skin-sticking black, the other in fluffy maroon, looked out.

'You're late,' said Arabella, ever the older sister. Her shoulder-length blonde hair seemed to crackle with accusation. 'You could have sent a text message or something. Where have you been?'

'You've brought company.' Sophia blinked rapidly, ridiculously long lashes fluttering madly as she did her best to hide her surprise. Her honey-gold hair was pulled back from her face, revealing her gamine features in a most appealing way.

Well, fine, so Chrissy didn't bring guys home as a rule. Neither did her sisters. Much. Although Bella had muttered something about some man the other day. Chrissy had taken no notice. If her older sister decided to get serious about anyone, they would hear about it.

Said sisters both stared at Nate, eyebrows raised, curiosity stamped on their gorgeous faces. No way would they let him simply disappear, now that Chrissy had turned up with him in tow. Her hopes of getting rid of Nate were smashed, although she would make one final effort, anyway.

'Arabella, Sophia, this is Henry's grandson, Nate Barrett. He was kind enough to take me to the hospital on the way home from work so I could see Henry.' She drew a quick breath and went on before either of them could interrupt. 'And you know you don't have to worry about me, Bella. I'm always careful.'

Except when I'm kissing attractive bosses in deserted hallways. 'I'm sure Nate has other plans now, though, so he won't be staying—'

'Pleased to meet you. Come in for a moment, do.' As though she hadn't even heard her sister, Soph grabbed Nate's arm and pulled him over the threshold and all but directly into her bright, fluffy arms.

Chrissy's mouth pinched. 'No need to strangle the man,' she muttered with ill grace. Soph probably *hadn't* listened. She had a way of not hearing things, of going off into her own little world.

Did this sudden warm welcome for Nate mean that her younger sister had her eye on him? Jealousy rumbled.

Bella stood back, arms folded, her modelling career very

much in evidence in her stance. Her fitted black catsuit added to the impression of strength and beauty.

She was very much *not* welcoming Nate with open arms, but some men liked that sort of challenge. It could be a ploy to attract Nate, anyway.

'So you're my sister's new boss,' Bella said.

Chrissy told herself to calm down. Her sisters *weren't* trying to bowl Nate over with their charms. They weren't like that.

Having got that piece of oversized resentment under control, she turned, still expecting to see Nate standing gobsmacked and silent. Either as a result of Soph's lovely charm, or Bella's incredible looks and self-contained poise.

Her sisters might not be throwing themselves at him, but that didn't change the fact that they were both worth more than a second glance.

He wasn't gobsmacked, though. He wasn't even looking at them. Instead, his gaze roved the living room. After a moment he turned to Bella, then Soph, nodded and thanked them for inviting him in. Polite. Bland. Not bowled over.

Something deep inside Chrissy relaxed its guard just the tiniest bit because of that fact. Nate had kissed *her*, had said he was attracted to *her*. Meeting her sisters hadn't distracted him.

The affair idea rose again. Looked even more appealing, damn his hide and her imagination and everything else she could think of to blame. She was mid-contemplation of some very irresponsible thoughts indeed, when Nate spoke again and ruined it all.

'Why don't you tell your sisters about the project you brought home?'

CHAPTER SIX

'OH, WE know all about the project.'

Before Chrissy could stop her, Soph babbled on about the crossword challenge they had planned for the evening, and about Henry's hopes of winning the contest.

Soph raised a guileless gaze to Nate's face. 'You'll stay, won't you? Another perspective on the questions can only help.'

That's just great, Sophia. Tell him everything, why don't you?

Chrissy glared, not that it did any good. Soph clearly believed Nate Barrett was no threat.

If only she knew. *The man is a ten scorch heatwave, and that's just for starters.*

'You're working on a crossword puzzle? That's what you brought home from the office?' Nate looked relieved, which was kind of weird.

Then his expression took on an edge of fire. His gaze narrowed and he leaned in to say, just for Chrissy, 'You could have told me, instead of letting me think…'

'Think what?' She threw her shoulders back. 'It wasn't my story to tell. Henry is very private about his crosswords.'

'Oh, Chrissy, shouldn't I have said anything?' Soph looked chagrined, belatedly. 'I thought, since Nate is Henry's grandson—'

'It doesn't matter.' Chrissy sighed and gave up.

To her sisters, Nate was simply Henry's grandson, who worked in the overseas part of the business. It wasn't Soph's fault if she assumed Nate would be welcome here to take part in this.

Soph couldn't know that Chrissy needed to get away from the man before she pounced on him and begged him to kiss her again, either.

'I don't want to cause my grandfather distress.' Nate's quiet words calmed her.

'I know. Sorry. It's a contest entry. Well, you'll see…' She hauled Henry's sheets of questions and answers out of her bag and tossed them onto the coffee-table. 'This is it.'

Bella riffled through the sheets of paper and groaned. 'So we need to cut up every question and answer and then start trying to match them? We have to work out ups and downs as well as everything else?'

'Eventually, yes. That's the purpose of the blank spread-sheet at the bottom of the pile. We can pencil things in as we work.'

'Why is this so important?' Nate lifted one of the sheets to examine it.

'It's Henry's proposed entry in the largest cryptic-crossword puzzle contest in Australia.' Chrissy grimaced. 'One thousand questions and answers. He's worked on it for almost two years. It just wouldn't be right if he had to miss out on entering when he's so close to finishing.'

Nate shook his head in disbelief. 'Surely he has a copy of the completed puzzle somewhere?'

'*Almost* completed, and yes, he had it on his computer, in a separate programme and file to the scrambled questions and answers.' Henry had been almost apoplectic when he realised he had destroyed that one and only copy. 'He managed to kill the file. We had a technician in, but it was no good. We'd lost it.'

'Back-up?' Nate asked, his expression incredulous.

She shrugged. 'I always do one, but Henry's a bit hit and miss about that.'

Soph turned toward the kitchen. 'I'll whip up some omelettes and a sticky date pudding. That'll cheer us up. I'm sure we've got the ingredients for both and I found this website of really easy recipes on the internet—'

'Actually, I'm really craving pizza.' Bella rubbed her flat tummy and adopted a desperate-for-junk-food expression. 'Cheese and pepperoni. Yum.'

'I could kill for a risotto from No. 71.' Chrissy should have let Bella handle it, but trying to head Soph off at the kitchen pass had become so ingrained that she couldn't stop herself.

'Let me order both.' Nate gave all three sisters a curious look, and drew out his cellphone. 'It would be my pleasure to buy you ladies dinner.'

In other circumstances, Chrissy would have argued. When the alternative was a night of indigestion from Soph's cooking, she provided Nate with phone numbers, tried not to feel guilty toward her sister, and made a prediction. 'I think we'll have to put our brains to good use tonight.'

By the time the pizza and risotto had arrived, there were chopped-up bits of crossword strewn from one end of the living room to the other, Soph was clearly charmed by Nate, and Bella had thawed sufficiently to bring out their best Chai tea and the china cups and saucers—her favoured means of relaxation.

'What do you think about this one?' Nate returned his empty cup to the saucer and held up a puzzle question.

Chrissy leaned forward in her chair to read it, and that leaning brought her almost into his lap where he sat on the floor with his back against the side of her seat.

She gave the puzzle question a cursory examination while

her pulse hammered in her ears. He had done that deliberately, just when she had started to relax and think she had things under control.

'I…uh…' She cleared her throat to try to rid it of that husky tremor. 'Actually, I have no idea.'

'Me neither.' He smiled a wolfish smile that her sisters couldn't see, and lifted the pizza box in front of her like a pagan love offering. 'Tempt you with a slice?'

'No, thank you.' *And you can stop tempting me with innuendo, too, you sneaky…villain of amorousness.*

He gave a low, sexy laugh and went on to converse with her sisters as though nothing out of the ordinary had happened. The glint in his eyes said differently.

Nate had blasted through all her rickety defences simply by smiling at her and offering her pizza. She was so much a goner!

It just went downhill from there. Sensual sighs. Casual touches that were anything but casual. The locking of gazes. Playful arguing that ended in a tussle against the lounge cushions as they fought over a single piece of puzzle.

It was all very subtle. Soph and Bella were absorbed, and Nate was good at masking his actions. But Chrissy hummed all over by the time her sisters decided to retire to bed.

'It's been hours.' Bella got to her feet and stretched. 'Pack it up. We'll tackle it again tomorrow.'

'Just a bit more.' Chrissy's gaze was locked on a puzzle question, but her senses were stuck on Nate and the warmth of shared body heat where their outer thighs pressed together in seeming innocence.

How long ago had she joined him to sit on the carpeted floor? Would he stay there with her when her sisters left the room?

You shouldn't want him to stay there. You should want him to leave, pronto, and you should forget he ever kissed you in the first place.

'Your choice, but don't whine to me if you're tired in the morning.' Bella cast Nate a thoughtful glance, then gave a sniff and left the room with Soph.

'I think your sister is wondering if she should be protective of you right now or not.' Nate's low words sent shivers over her. Made her think of all the ways she could get into trouble with a man on the floor in the middle of a paper-strewn living room.

'Bella's the eldest. She felt obligated to watch out for all of us when…' She trailed off, not about to discuss her parents' abrupt removal to the other side of the world.

Instead, she stared again at Henry's clue, *Wheels avoid un-married floral posy (7) (4) (5) (movie)*, and willed herself to be calm and unaffected.

And then she looked up. Nate watched her as though he might like to have her for dessert instead of the sticky date pudding Soph had offered.

Suddenly, dessert seemed like a wonderful idea. Provided it involved Nate and kisses on the floor.

Next thing you will *throw yourself at him!* Which really couldn't be allowed to happen.

'*Driving Miss Daisy,*' she blurted, and dived for the pile of now much mangled, cut-up answers strewn across the sofa. All her ideas of playing the *femme fatale* disintegrated in a bout of well-deserved nervous tension.

'I'll bet there's a match for that somewhere.'

'Christianna.'

Her full name. For the second time. On Nate's lips it sounded so good.

'Yes,' she babbled. 'We all got the full treatment with our names. Arabella, Christianna and Sophia. That's *Soh-fee-ah*, as in *Loren*. Our parents weren't into ordinariness, although in the end they should have called me something plain. Like

Jane. Not that I'm saying Janes are plain because clearly that would just be silly.'

She ground to a halt. 'I'm sure you're not interested. They're just names, after all.' Names handed out by parents who had later found the trauma of raising two reasonably acceptable daughters and one severe disappointment too much to be endured.

'Where are your parents now?' One side of his mouth had kicked up, but now he sobered. Waited for her answer. Looked as though he really cared one way or the other.

Chrissy wanted to blurt out the whole horrible truth. All she said was, 'They're overseas.' As far as she knew, it was still the case.

'Well, my, will you look at the time?' She abandoned the cut-up crossword answers, sprang to her feet and made an elaborate show of glancing at her wrist.

Her gambit would have worked better if she had had a watch on. 'You must be exhausted. No doubt you're wishing we hadn't kept you so long, although we made reasonable progress if I do say so myself.'

'You're gabbling.' He stood, clasped her hand and tugged her forward. 'It's sexy. Watching you eat risotto is sexy, too. And the way you stretch the mozzarella on the pizza slice, then wrap it around your finger—'

Sexy? Gabbling? He had watched her eat and found that appealing, too? That certainly put a cork in her babble. *And* wrecked her filigree-thin resistance to him. 'Ah—'

'I want to stay, Chrissy, but I don't think that would be smart.' His smile had a hint of self-deprecation in it. 'I'm not sure I could be a gentleman.'

'Oh. Right. Um…' He was halfway to the door before she caught up physically. Mentally, she was still somewhere back in *Can I match this crossword clue?*

Tell the truth. It had nothing to do with cryptic puzzling.

She was deep in reacting to his comment about her—according to him—sexy ramblings and munchings, and to his clearly spoken desire to remain here with her, even though he believed it would be unwise.

That was the reality of it.

'Do I want to know what you're thinking?' Nate stroked his fingers across her cheek, just as he had done the first day they met. 'Or would I wish I hadn't asked?'

'You'd wish…' This time she knew his touch. That fact should have reduced its impact. Instead, it increased her longing for more than a touch. Even though she couldn't trust him to want her for more than a moment.

He caressed her neck once, then dropped his hand and stepped away. 'I had no right to question you about the contents of your bag. I'm sorry.'

She wanted his touch again. Shouldn't have, but did. 'Why did you question me?'

For a moment he hesitated. 'It was nothing. Just a stupid thought, but Chrissy, if you're in some sort of trouble…' He broke off and clamped his jaw.

She frowned. 'I don't know what you mean.'

'Never mind. I'll pick you up in the morning. Ten o'clock. We'll find out if Henry's feeling any better.' He turned and left without a backward glance.

I won't go to the hospital with him. It's not like he invited me. 'I don't like dictatorial males.'

'Same.' Soph's hand tightened on a section of her hair.

'Ow.' Chrissy rubbed her scalp. 'What are you doing?'

Soph eased her movements. 'Sorry. I'll be more careful.'

The doorbell rang. Chrissy's body jerked reactively, and Soph pushed her back down onto the stool. 'Wonder who that is. *I'm* certainly not expecting anyone.'

'Neither am I.' Bella stopped her Pilates exercises, shrugged her newly created silk wrap on over her exercise gear and headed for the door.

Chrissy knew who would be on the other side of the door. She suddenly panicked, and motioned Bella over to the make-shift hair salon in the kitchen while making frantic shushing motions at her.

Bella rolled her eyes, but stalked closer on silent feet. The doorbell rang again.

'What's the problem?' Bella whispered.

'It's Nate. He's come to take me to see Henry.' Chrissy strained to sit still while Soph continued to work on her hair. 'Tell him I'm not here.'

'Well, that makes a lot of sense.' Bella's eyebrows went up. Then down into a frown. 'All right. Whatever you say.' She strode to the door and opened it a crack. 'Hello.'

Nate's deep voice drifted into the apartment. 'I'm here for Chrissy. We made arrangements to visit Henry this morning.'

Chrissy fought the urge to drop to her knees and crawl using the furniture as a shield until she reached the safety of the bedroom she shared with Soph. What on earth had come over her? Five minutes ago she had intended to go with Nate, just to tell him to steer clear of tempting her.

Now she wanted to stay right away from Mr Nate Barrett of the kissy lips and sexy smile and—

'Shall I come in to wait?' The calm, determined tone came clearly to her despite the fact that her head was currently smothered in Sophia's green and black frog-clad bosom, while her hair was being tugged this way and that by her busy, determined hands.

Soph bashed her elbow on a cupboard and gave a soft, ir-ritated snarl. 'Hold still, will ya? I'm almost done.'

'That's what you said an hour ago.' Chrissy strained to get

a glimpse of Nate through the crack of door Bella had opened when he arrived. Why didn't Bella just get rid of him?

'Chrissy's, uh, not available,' Bella said, and tried to close the door again.

'Can't you finish it, Soph?' Chrissy wriggled on the kitchen stool.

'I'm almost done, and what's your problem, anyway? Why don't you want to go with him?' With a flourish, Soph stood back. 'There. You look great. I think. No. No, really. You do.'

Chrissy bit back a doubtful comment. Soph was trying so hard to be a great hairdresser. She had to practise on someone. 'How many colours did you say you used?'

But Soph had disappeared into the bathroom, muttering about not being caught dead in her nightwear.

Unable to contain her curiosity about the conversation going on between Nate and Bella, Chrissy edged toward the door. Bella had that stiff look and, from the peek she got of him, Nate seemed to be chafing where he stood on the front step.

As Chrissy approached, Nate spoke again. 'Did you make the robe you're wearing?' The topic of Bella's sewing had arisen last night during the crossword-a-thon. In fact, a lot of topics had arisen. Soph was a bit of a blabbermouth. 'It's—ah—it's very colourful.'

'Yes, I made it. The fabric was a gift from Chrissy. I thought she might have told you.' Bella's gaze narrowed. 'Why do you ask?'

'No reason.' It was then that Chrissy saw that Nate had the toe of one shoe jammed in the doorway, and realised he was making small talk in an effort to get Bella to let him inside.

He inched his foot forward. 'I know you said Chrissy wasn't here, but I thought I heard her voice.'

'Chrissy isn't…that is, she's sort of….' Bella flapped a thin, elegant hand. No doubt she could feel Chrissy breathing down her neck from behind, and she hated any sort of prevarication. 'Sophia is still in her pyjamas, so it wouldn't be appropriate—'

'It's OK.' Chrissy tugged the door out of Bella's hands and opened it wider. 'I've decided I _will_ go with him.' This nonsense had to end. The man had all but sent her cowering to her room, for heaven's sake. 'I've got a few things to say. Might as well get them over with.'

Bella glared. 'Fine, but I wish you'd make up your mind.' She turned and disappeared inside.

That left Nate and Chrissy, facing each other across the now fully opened doorway.

Nate stared. And stared some more. At her hair, draped over her shoulders and falling down her back in a riot of multi-coloured waves that ended at her waist.

She bristled with suppressed anticipation of a negative comment. Something along the lines of, _If it was a little longer, you would look like Cousin Itt in neon._

'Your hair.' He almost whispered it.

'What about it?' She tugged at the fawn crocheted top that covered her blouse and waited. The purple, green and orange highlights Soph had so painstakingly added to her hair this morning made her feel like a misplaced rainbow. They were temporary, but that didn't make them any less striking.

'Dear God. You. You, ah…' He gestured toward her hair. 'That's… It's longer than I'd guessed it would be.'

Not exactly an insult, and what about the colour change?

'I like it long.' In truth, she had a love-hate relationship with her hair. If only it had been straight, like Soph's and Bella's, instead of uncontrollably curly like an electrified dish-mop. Or if it had been some shade of blonde, instead of mud-brown.

Her mother had stopped taking her to hairdressers when

she was eight. Now Chrissy figured if she cut her hair short it would simply frizz more, so she kept it long. Usually she just tucked it up and tried to forget it.

But with Nate looking at her like this, she was very aware of the flow of it over her shoulders and down her back. It felt…sensual.

'There's no time to change it.' She turned and snatched her coat and bag from inside. Her hair whipped out around her. 'Besides, Sophia's on the last legs of a hairdressing course. She wanted to practise her colours. It would have hurt her feelings if I'd braided it so nobody could see her work.'

'I'm glad you didn't braid it.' The sincerity of his statement was unmistakable. The glitter of male awareness in his gaze was too blatant to be denied.

Every strand of her hair tightened against her scalp, until she felt as though simply his *look* had touched it, stroked it, taken that stroking feeling back to her skin and radiated it there.

Just that easily, he tipped her off the cliff again. 'We should get on the road or we'll be late.' Irritated at the huskiness of her tone, she slung the piece of tangled macramé that served as today's shoulder bag over one arm, her coat over the other and gave him what she hoped was a frosty look.

Surely a rational request to cease and desist attracting her would take care of the problem?

So, say it.

'I'm glad you called for me this morning, Nate. The drive will be the perfect opportunity for us to…'

He didn't appear to be listening. Instead, he stared at her mouth with a glazed expression. One of his hands reached out and stroked a long length of her wildly curling hair. He inhaled sharply and his hand tightened.

'*Park on the way…fog up the windows a bit maybe,*' she thought she heard him mutter.

A glance beyond him into the street revealed clear weather. 'I don't see any fog. But I'm looking forward to settling a few issues that have been on my mind since last night.'

'Ah.' A flush bloomed across the bridge of his nose and spanned across each cheekbone. It wasn't an embarrassed kind of flush. Rather, it was a flush that made the very pores of her skin tighten.

How could he do that to her, just by reflecting a purely physical awareness?

'Sorry.' He seemed to forcibly pull his thoughts together. His face gradually shifted out of the realms of sensual awareness into something more urbane, but equally watchful. 'My mind drifted. What was it that you said?'

'Try listening properly. You'll be amazed how well it works.' She marched out the door—fortunately he got out of her way before she collided with him—and charged at the stairs.

Then she remembered she didn't want Nate to observe the Behemoth Barge. Nope, not letting that happen again. She stopped. Waved a hand. 'After you.'

'Ladies first.' The growl of his words wrapped itself over her. Layered her in warm heat. 'I insist.'

'Fine.' She adjusted her glasses and scooted down the stairwell with the finesse of a mouse in full ship-escaping scurry.

Behind her, Nate moaned softly. She refused to contemplate the possible meanings of that moan. Other than that maybe he had gout in his toe and descending the stairs bothered it.

When they reached his car, she tossed her handbag onto the floor and got in. Nate climbed aboard, too.

As he turned the key in the ignition she moved directly to the first point, as far as she was concerned, of this morning's excursion.

Aside from getting to see Henry, or course. 'I'm here because I want to talk to you, not because you kissed me, drove me mad all yesterday evening then coerced me into going to the hospital with you today.'

'Actually, I thought it would make it easier—'

'No. Don't interrupt me.' No way would she let his charismatic charm get to her in the light of day. Not now that she had taken the time to examine all the things she had allowed to go wrong yesterday and last night.

Like losing control so he could kiss her while she just stood there and allowed it to happen.

And gave back as good as she got.

OK, fine. She may have done that, but Nate had charmed her so that she forgot what he was all about. Forgot he was an abandoner!

'All right, Chrissy. I'll listen.' He didn't sound pleased, but he agreed, and moved the car onto the street.

'Good. First, I want your assurance that you won't breathe a word to Henry about us trying to get his crossword entry finished in time to enter it into the contest.'

She reasoned that this was, indeed, important. Henry would worry over it too much, would want to join in and help them put it all together.

'Your secret is safe with me,' Nate drawled, and took the exit lane.

In moments they were cruising a less cluttered road. If it had been a movie he would have put the top down, and she would have whipped out a scarf and sunglasses and laughed gaily as the fresh air buffeted her.

But this was Victoria in the middle of winter. It was way too cold to do anything but snuggle inside and enjoy the car's heater.

Jeez. It's a trip to see your boss at a hospital. There is not a single romantic thing about it, either real or imagined.

Romantic, perhaps not. But the sensuality lingered, just waiting to catch her if she didn't remain vigilant against it. That vigilance needed to be given voice. Right now. 'You're not to touch me again.'

Nate's expression flattened slightly, but that was all. 'By touch you, do I assume you mean—?'

'No more touching, no more kissing, no more missy moo-moo eyes.' The latter was for her own benefit, but nevertheless she thought her demands clarified things. 'We're colleagues. I want a professional relationship, and absolutely nothing else.'

She didn't owe him any further explanation. Instead, she fixed him with a gimlet gaze that would have done Bella proud and demanded his agreement. 'Do I have your word on it?'

CHAPTER SEVEN

'I DISCOVERED that Margaret *was* trying to use Janice Deanne to ferret out information about the company.' Nate growled the piece of information as he waited with Chrissy by the lifts. Any conversation, even one about Henry's wife, was better than an aching, loaded silence.

Four days ago he had given his word to Chrissy. In his own way. He had agreed not to touch her until she made it clear she wanted it. The statement had been arrogant and ego-inflated. A knee-jerk reaction to her rejection of him, even though he had told himself he should be rejecting her, too.

Now Nate was fed-up. Irritated on so many levels he had lost count.

The investigators hadn't discovered anything of use at the docks. Henry had nagged until Nate was forced to have him shifted to his home with round-the-clock nursing care. At least Margaret wasn't there. According to Henry, his wife had made a spur-of-the-moment decision to visit Tasmania.

'I hope you weren't hard on Janice.' Chrissy's words jolted him back to the present. 'She's a good woman and has always been loyal to the company. I can't imagine why she would want anything to do with Margaret, actually.'

On the surface, Chrissy's comments were calm, unlike her pithy reaction to his statement on the weekend that he wouldn't touch her until she asked for it.

Her terse response had been followed by a death glare, and then she had retreated into a scrupulously polite mode of behaviour that had driven Nate slowly and surely around the bend. 'I need a damned replacement.'

'You didn't fire Janice?'

'No.' He paused, his thoughts on whether Margaret could somehow be behind the accounting discrepancies that were coming to light within the company. 'Janice had already realised Margaret was only acting nice to pump her for information, and had ended the so-called friendship.'

'Oh.' Her tone softened. 'Well, I'm relieved to hear that Janice is still with us.'

Her approval pleased him out of all proportion.

'So, is there anything else we need to take care of before we can leave?' Her tone held no accusation, but he heard the hint of weariness. She shifted slightly and the faint scent of herbs came from her hair, mixed with her body warmth to intoxicate him.

'No. We're finished.' Another five minutes in the same space as her and he just might lose control, anyway.

Knowing there wasn't a single person in this office capable of taking over from his grandfather didn't help. He was stuck here until he found a replacement from further afield, and selling that person to Henry would be even harder than selling Henry on someone local.

Selling himself on not wanting Chrissy was Nate's toughest challenge yet. So far he was failing miserably.

Chrissy sighed. 'I'm glad there's nothing else to be done, actually, because I'm bushed.'

Thunder rumbled outside the building, reverberated inside

him. He was tired, too, but also oddly energised. 'There's going to be one hell of a storm.'

'I don't like violent weather.' She shuddered.

If he could simply kiss her again, just once, no holds barred, to the point of satiation. Then surely this deep-seated curiosity would be laid to rest.

'It's got to be the damned hair,' he grated, and jabbed again at the button for the lift.

It was eleven pm. The cleaners didn't come in until early morning. Aside from him and Chrissy, the building was deserted. He should focus on getting back to the cottage. A shower and bed. Those were things to contemplate with real pleasure.

There would be even more pleasure if you shared the shower and bed with Chrissy, a sly voice suggested inside his head—not for the first time.

As though sensing his thoughts, Chrissy cut a glance toward him. The big owl glasses slid down her pert little nose, just inviting him to take them off and press kisses all over her face. Her hair looked like a ruffled bird's nest. As if it had known the touch of a man's hands. That attracted him, too.

She lifted her free hand and prodded at the nut-brown mass. 'Is there something wrong with my hair?'

Only the fact that now I've seen it down, I imagine it that way every time I see you. Imagine it flowing through my hands, brushing against my skin...

'Nope, but I think it's picked up some static from the storm.' He would be happy to be jolted by that static any time. 'I'd forgotten Melbourne weather had so many moods and faces.'

'Sort of like a skilful lover,' she said, and turned an instant fiery red from the neck up. 'I mean, a storm can, ah, achieve just about anything in terms of displaying its power. Um, that is—'

'Quite right.' He snapped the words to stop her from going

any further because he didn't want to imagine her in the arms of a lover.

You'd willingly imagine it if you were that lover.

He studied the blush that covered not only face and neck, but also the small V of chest he could see above her blouse. Acknowledged the inexperience that blush revealed. Suffered an instant, urgent need to discover how far the wave of heat had spread.

'Actually, Christianna, your comment just now was rather open to interpretation.' He didn't know why he goaded her. Maybe he just enjoyed torturing himself, but did she really feel nothing for him now? 'Are you trying to renege on your demand for a solely professional relationship? Is that what your double-edged statement was about?'

'The only thing I want to communicate to you,' she said in a chilled tone, 'is that the work day is finished and so, therefore, has our association for the day. The rest was a nervous blurt, if you must know.'

'I don't want to make you nervous.' He meant that. But he *did* want to make her cry out his name while she looked into his eyes and melted away. Would the idea of *that* make her nervous?

This was insane. Maybe *he* was insane. Being back here in Melbourne was messing with his mind. Working in the home office again, among the old familiar faces, made him nostalgic.

Yes, that was it. He was suffering from a bout of nostalgia. *So, you'd like to live a lovely, nostalgic life with her in Henry's hideaway cottage for the next fifty years?*

'Hell, no,' he said so vehemently that Chrissy jumped beside him.

'Sorry. Just thinking out loud.' The lift dinged open—finally—and they stepped inside.

Chrissy began to fidget as soon as the doors closed. 'It's

not that *you* make me nervous. Why would you? I don't like the way this storm feels, that's all.'

Cut down to size by a slip of a girl in a frilly wrap-over blouse, black cardigan and bulky, ugly speckled coat.

She gave a shiver. 'I'll just be glad to get home.'

Home, and away from him. She had wanted that distance from the start, despite the attraction between them. She'd thought she knew him. Had decided his fate before they ever met. Why condemn him so thoroughly? Why be so swift to reject the possibility of getting to know each other while he was here?

You mean the quick affair she's already rejected.

The collar of his shirt felt too tight all of a sudden. He ran a finger beneath it. 'Thank you for working late today. I'm sorry I had to throw so much your way, but there were other things I needed to do.'

Such as stretching his search for a replacement so he could leave. They stepped out into the car park.

'I *am* used to it, you know.' Theirs were the only cars left in the car park. They paused at the midpoint between them, and she turned her attention fully upon him.

For one mind-blanking moment, he thought she meant she was accustomed to indulging in short-term affairs. The thought of it made him seethe with all sorts of fraught feelings—most of which fell into the possessive, totally irrational disapproving category—until he realised he had misunderstood.

'You mean you're used to a lot of responsibility at Montbank Shipping.'

'Yes.' A small frown formed between her eyes. 'What else would I mean?'

'How much of the workload did my grandfather push your way?' He asked the question, but his thoughts asked other questions. Wanted other answers.

'It wasn't that he didn't want to work.' Fondness tinged her smile. 'Henry was always working.' She gave that gentle smile again. 'It's just that sometimes the work was unrelated to Montbank Shipping. When he got really engrossed, I'd have to take care of most things until he came back down to earth.'

'Like the crossword puzzle.' The mention of it brought memories of the night they had shared with her sisters in their cosy apartment. Of the kiss that had preceded it, and the need to be close to her that he had experienced afterward. That need had stuck.

'We expect to have the crossword finished by the end of the coming weekend.' A crash of thunder reverberated overhead. She concealed her flinch almost perfectly. 'Bella and Soph have been a great help. Once it's done, we'll tell Henry and it can go into the contest.'

Another crash, this one closer. The lights flickered. Nate's protective instincts surged. He may not be able to ravish her the way he wanted to, but he could keep her safe from this. 'The storm is worsening. Let me drive you to your apartment.'

'I have Gertie to get me there.' Her glance moved between their two vehicles. 'But thanks for the offer.'

It hadn't actually been an offer, more of an insistence. That need to keep her from harm, real or imagined, fuelled his frustration—with himself, with her. 'Then I'll drive you home in your car and I'll get a taxi to the cottage.'

'I'll be perfectly—'

'Fine?' Not on his shift. Not in this weather. As though to support him, thunder crashed in a long, deafening roar over their heads and rain bucketed down in the street visible through the entry-exit area. 'You see? You can't possibly go out in that.'

'Oh, yes, I can.' Her voice quavered slightly, but her chin

was up. 'Other people manage to drive in rough weather. Why shouldn't I?'

'I didn't mean that.' Her limited experience behind the wheel didn't worry him. Overly. Unless he dwelt on it, but… '*Nobody* should have to be out in this.'

The lights in the car park went out. Aside from the occasional car inching by in the torrential rain outside, and the scant street lighting and building lights, all went dim. This time her flinch was not so well-concealed. She moved instinctively closer to him.

Just like that, his senses roared. Before he could act on that response, she jerked her shoulders back and put several paces of space between them.

'We should go before this gets any worse. I'll see you tomorrow morning.'

'Wait.' In sync with his demand, the lights in the building flickered out, too, as did all the discernible lights outside the area. With the street momentarily empty of cars, they were pitched into utter darkness by what appeared to be at least a localised blackout, possibly something more widespread.

He swore, sharply and fluently, and heard her draw a sharp breath.

'Would you help me to my car?' Her words were stiff. 'I'm…not very good in the dark.'

'I can't see, either.' But he could hear, could sense her presence to his left and could smell her light, familiar scent.

I could find her in a snowstorm even without that elusive scent. She's like a homing beacon to me. I would find her anywhere.

He sucked up a startled breath. Chrissy was no homing beacon, and he was no marooned life form looking for someone to guide him to safe harbour!

Yet he wanted her so much. The last thing he needed

was a night in close proximity to her. He wasn't sure his resistance could meet the challenge.

Would the blackout last all night? It would probably depend on how widespread it was. His frustration flared into incautious words. 'Great. Now we're trapped here together for who knows how long. Could it get any worse? This is about the last thing I need.'

As soon as he spoke, he wished the words unsaid, but the damage was done.

'If you don't want to assist me to my car,' she enunciated in frozen tones, 'I'll get there myself. I certainly don't want to be any sort of burden to you.'

Damn it. He hadn't felt this inept since high school. He softened his voice and reached for her hand, found it in the darkness and clasped the chilled fingers. 'Let's get to my car, first of all. It's the closest.'

'Fine.' She tugged her hand free and clasped his arm with stiff fingers. 'When we reach it, you can shine your lights so I can find my way to Gertie. Being trapped any place with you is the last thing I need, too, you know!'

'I didn't mean to upset you—'

'That's perfectly all right.' He sensed the stiffness in her body at his side. 'I'm reassured, actually, that you've finally come to your senses and accepted there should be nothing between us.'

'There's nothing wrong with my senses and never has been. You're the one who's been fighting your own nature and throwing down ridiculous dictates.' It was because his senses wouldn't let up that he felt so irritable now.

'I don't dictate,' she huffed. 'I request in a polite and rational manner. There's nothing ridiculous about me.'

'No, there isn't. Actually, I think I'm the fool.' He guided her toward his car in silence, cursing the darkness that made movement slow. 'Here it is.'

He unlocked his car and looked at her in the glow of the dim interior light. Fire and anger burned in her face, in her eyes. Every shred of sense told him he should see her to her car, then spend however long their incarceration lasted safely tucked into his. Far away from her.

Except that, even in anger, she was so beautiful she took his breath away. And that her unease with the storm and the darkness clearly showed despite her efforts to disguise it.

'Thank you.' She stepped back, the tremble in her voice barely detectable. 'If you'll shine your headlights—'

'You can't drive away, Chrissy. We can't get out at all. We're trapped here until the blackout is over.' He could have finessed the bald truth. Instead, he simply sounded frustrated again. 'With the electricity off, we're stuck. The boom gates—'

'We can't be trapped. Surely we can...' The pitch of her voice was higher than usual. It revealed her tension and unease.

But there was a different kind of unease in her eyes. Only one thing brought that particular look to a woman. Despite what she had said on Saturday and her behaviour since, she still wanted him.

'The only way out would be to try to smash through the boom gates with one of our cars.' His harsh words reflected his state of mind.

'We're really stuck here until the lights come back on, then.' She pinned on a brave face that stripped away his anger. 'I guess we can't get back into the building, either.'

'The keypad for the lift is electronic. There's a stairwell escape from inside the building to the parking lot, but it's—'

'Locked from the inside.' She rubbed her hands together in a nervous gesture. 'Well, I guess I'll just sit in my car until the lights come back on. I hope I can get a reception on my cellphone down here so I can let Bella and Soph know what's happened.'

CHAPTER EIGHT

'I DON'T want to leave you alone in your car for who knows how long.' Nate's words were as dark as the storm, but underlaid with a gentleness revealed by the transient touch of his hand against hers.

They stood in the arc of light thrown by his car's opened door. Chrissy wanted to remain angry toward him. Instead, his caring warmed her. She understood his frustration, too, for she shared it. His words earlier had simply been a snarled attempt to keep need at bay.

That need in him fuelled hers and her hunger warred with her caution. Emotions polarised, she held back a moan. 'I...don't want to be alone.' She shouldn't have admitted it. But this—the storm, the blackout, the two of them trapped as though they were alone in the world—was too much.

'Damn it, Chrissy.' He didn't move, but it seemed as though all of him drew closer to her. 'I'm on a thin line, here. That didn't help me.'

Inexplicably, hearing it, knowing she had voiced her feelings, released her and she stopped worrying quite so much. She gestured toward the other side of the car park. 'I have some things in my car that might be useful. If we're going to be here awhile, I'll be happy to share them.'

'We should wait the storm out in my car. It's roomier.'
Despite his words, she noticed his hesitation.

'We can just talk.' The need to reassure him was alien, but
somehow seemed right just now. 'Or doze or something.
Look on the bright side—at least we had dinner brought in
earlier.'

'Yeah. I guess that's something good, and we can do that.
Talk, and stuff.' His voice held residual disbelief, but he flicked
the convertible's headlights on and they moved to her car.

She sent a quick text message to Bella—*Blackout. Stuck
at work. Don't worry*. Then leaned into the car.

'OK. Let's see what I've got here.' She retrieved two
Afghan lap rugs from the backseat, a red cushion in the shape
of a heart and a bottle of water.

Nate's brows rose with each addition to their pile of
goodies. 'Not a bad haul.'

Still feeling a bit embarrassed about that heart-shaped
cushion—a Valentine's day gift bought for herself a couple
of years ago—she muttered something she hoped was appropriate and made for his car.

'Do you have any necessities hidden away in your car?'
She asked the question to cover the return of her nervousness
as they shucked off their coats and climbed into the convertible. The leather bench seat was slippery. She almost slid
right into his lap. 'Somehow I don't think of necessities when
I look at this car, though.'

'What do you think of?'

'Oh, you know.' She flapped the hand that didn't hold the
heart cushion.

*Sin in all its most tempting, Nate-related formats is mostly
what I think of when I think of this car.*

'Ah, I think of, ah, a past era. Drive-in movies.' Necking.
Kissing you. 'That sort of thing.'

He grinned and held the blankets up. The expression on his face told her he had read her thoughts. 'We'll pool these and our coats for warmth.'

'Are you sure we need to share? We could sort of huddle into one each….'

'We do need to huddle.' He agreed readily enough, but with a gleam in his eyes. 'We just need to do it together, that's all. But don't worry. You said we should talk or snooze. I'm game for that if you are.'

She gulped air while her heart pounded and her palms moistened and blood rushed to her head. 'Oh, sure, I don't mind sharing body heat, and, um, talking and stuff. Just how much heat do you think we'll be making between us though?'

He slammed his door shut, plunging them into darkness. 'Come this way a little, Christianna, and I'll shift, too. We'll meet in the middle and discover the answer to your question for ourselves.'

'I won't kiss you.' It was a last, pathetic effort to hold back. To prevent her feelings from betraying her. To prevent herself from kissing the man senseless. And making herself senseless in the process.

'I didn't ask you to.' She felt him shift in the darkness, heard the faint rustle of his clothing against the leather seat and caught the scent of day-old cologne from his skin.

'O-OK.' She removed her glasses and laid them on the dashboard. Then shuffled across the seat. Felt the softness of the Afghans close over her as he tugged her against his side and covered them both. The weight of their coats followed.

The red cushion slid onto the seat. She had Nate's body to warm her, and the rise and fall of his chest beneath her hand for comfort.

With a slight gasp, she raised her hand away from where it had unknowingly settled.

Nate caught it and returned it to its position against his chest. 'Whatever you want, Chrissy. However little or however much, any way, any time.'

Did he realise how little restraint she had right now? She wanted to bury her head against his shoulder and soak him in through her skin. Her head drooped toward that enticing shoulder. She tried to lift it.

He put an arm over her shoulders and tucked her against his side, making the decision for her. 'I haven't tried to hide what I want, but this can still just be the two of us keeping warm in a car while we wait out a storm and a blackout. It doesn't have to be more than that. You're the one who chooses. OK?'

'I don't think I know if I'm OK any more.' But they talked in low voices in a desultory fashion and eventually the combination of soft Afghans and hard, warm Nate lulled her into a state of contentment.

Her eyelashes fluttered and came to rest against her cheeks and with a quiet, confused sigh she drifted into the first layers of sleep. Aware but not fully conscious, she snuggled automatically closer as Nate's arm tightened around her and he bent his head to nuzzle her face.

When his fingers moved in her hair, releasing it from its pins, she mumbled and sighed again in pleasure as the restraints were taken away.

'Your hair is so beautiful. I wonder why you don't wear it loose more often.' Nate spoke aloud, aware that Chrissy was too far into sleep now to register his words. It was just as well, because he didn't know how much longer he could have continued the pretence of being in control of his desire for her.

He wound a handful of those long brown tresses around his fist, and her face pressed into his neck. Her hand still rested against his chest, and he wanted it there. Wanted every connection with her that he could get.

Christianna Gable, if there was any way in the world that I could stay with a woman, I think that woman might very well be you.

The thought slipped through his defences. He shifted restlessly, but didn't let go of her. After a long hesitation, he laid the seat back gently so they could rest easier.

'Mmm. Nate.' She snuggled into his side like a contented kitten, sending his body into instant overdrive.

He stared into the darkness, told his body to quiet and finally, in the early hours, when the city outside was at its quietest, the storm reduced to steady rain and her hair still fisted in his hand, he slept.

Chrissy woke to the sensation of Nate's warm, sensual mouth pressed over hers, their kiss already deep and hot and greedy. Her senses awash with need, her defences all but non-existent, she moaned and clenched her hands on his shoulders.

They were lying down, their bodies melded in a needy press. As she opened her eyes a car passed by outside, illuminating just enough for her to see the heat in Nate's sensual blue eyes. She should stop this. But right now, in Nate's embrace, she couldn't remember why.

She managed instead just a single word. 'Nate?'

'I'm here.' Darkness enveloped them fully once again. His hands shaped her spine, and his voice deepened even more. 'If I'm dreaming, I don't want to wake up.'

'The storm has finished.' No rain, no thunder. Just her inner turmoil for company.

'Has the storm finished?' His soft question shivered down her spine. 'Because I still want you, and there's nothing calm or tranquil about that.'

'Right, um, well, I guess…' They had gravitated to each

other in mutual desire, and now she wanted to let that desire take them further.

This will never happen again, so if I want to kiss him, why shouldn't I? If I want to do more than kiss him—her breath caught—*why shouldn't I?*

When he pushed her hair back off her face, she made her decision. She could have this one experience with him, and then let it go. Let him go. After all, it wasn't as if she loved him or anything.

Forcing aside a sudden uneasiness, she curved her arm around his mid-section and raised her face to his.

His mouth covered hers in a swift, hungry press. The touch of his lips both demanded and gave as he drew her deep into the circle of his arms.

Nate...I want you to care for me as I care for you.

The thought rose, and again she squashed it. Later. She would worry about that later.

'Sweet Christianna. I've wanted this.' He rolled, taking her with him until she lay almost beneath him. Her heart almost stopped, then fluttered to deep, turbulent life as the kiss changed, deepened even more.

'You have no idea how much I want you.' His words brushed against her ear, whisper-soft, thrilling, empowering.

'I want you, too.' *More than I can say. More than I'm willing to admit.*

'Chrissy.' He moaned her name against her mouth, every muscle in his body locked, fighting need, fighting for control. 'I think I should have insisted you leave your glasses on. You tempt me too much this way. I want to make love to you...'

He broke off. Took a moment to retrieve the Afghans and coats they had lost in their distraction and tuck them over her. Protection against the chilly air.

'If you want to make love to me, then why don't you?' In her heart it was the only decision she could make.

'Sweet lord, Chrissy. If you mean that…'

'I do.' It was all she could say, and the darkness shrouded her feelings, made it easy to say it.

He let out a low, growling rumble and bent to lave the flesh just beneath her ear with his tongue.

Shivers enveloped her.

'You humble me.' Nate nipped Chrissy's skin with his teeth. His entire body was on red alert, utterly sensitised to hers. 'You should stop me, if you don't want this. I realise you might not have thought about what you're doing, about what you said—'

'I've thought.' She tugged him closer. Made it clear what she had thought about. 'I'm sure.'

'Ah, dear lord.' He buried his face in her hair, fighting for the control that had never deserted him with a woman. Pressed his body against hers for a single moment of mind-numbing relief that caused an equal amount of frustrated pain. Yet he couldn't stop. 'Open your mouth to me.'

'You do the same.' Her throaty directive fired his senses.

Tenderness gave way to a deeper need that rocked his world. Made him want to shout that she was his. That they belonged together and principles and scruples and every other impediment be damned.

All rational thought left him at that moment. Chased out by need and hunger and a sensual greediness that shocked him it its raw, elemental intensity. He had to have her. Had to make her his.

The storm of emotion that raged through him at the thought cut off his breath. He didn't understand it, and now wasn't the time to try to work it out.

His arms locked around her. 'Don't move. Don't change anything. I want you here. Right as you are.'

'I don't want to move, Nate. I...it feels too good.'

When their mouths met, he understood the sense of welcome he had felt upon waking with her in his arms. She made him feel as though he belonged, and he wanted that feeling of belonging. Rashly welcomed it.

With shaking hands, he tugged her blouse from the waistband of her skirt. His fingers swept her midriff with long strokes. 'You're so beautiful.'

'I'm out of proportion. Thin and not very shapely on top—'

'You're perfect.' His hands rose, cupped the lovely softness of her breasts. 'Absolutely perfect in every way there is.' He caressed her back, her bottom, her thighs. Clenched his teeth as desire begged for fulfilment. 'Beautiful everywhere.'

'I want to touch you, too.' Her hands rose to the buttons of his shirt. 'May I?'

'Yes.' *Oh, please, yes!*

Her hands on his bare chest made him tingle with longing. 'You're— I need you. Let me—'

'I want it to be you, Nate. Only you.'

At her words, his mind whispered a warning, but his body refused to heed it. Locked to her, he couldn't make himself let go.

But he hesitated for just a moment, and in that moment the lights in the car park flickered on. He could see her clearly. The innocence, the determination, the awakened look of a woman awaiting fulfilment.

'No.' He forced the denial from tight lips. 'What was I doing? This shouldn't have happened.'

How could he have let things get this far, when he knew he wouldn't stay? Self-recrimination filled him with bitter regret.

'What do you mean?' Confusion rang in her voice. The beginnings of the truth clouded her eyes. 'Nate, we don't have to stop. We can—'

'Don't say it.' He dredged the words out of the shred of control that remained. Growled them in a tone roughened by self-blame and residual hunger.

Every fibre of his being argued that she was *his*. His to take, his to give to, *his*. But she wasn't. He had no right to try to hold her.

She's not yours. She never has been, even if she did make it sound as though she wanted this just as much as you do.

'Chrissy.' *I'm sorry. I want to make love to you, and to keep you always because I know it's what you would need. But I can't.*

Emotion knotted in his throat. He buttoned his shirt. Tried not to think of the feel of her hands on him, of how much he missed her touch, even now. 'This was a mistake. It shouldn't have happened. I can't... I'm not staying. I didn't mean for you to think...'

'I—I see.' Her face blanched.

He tried to explain. To help her to understand. 'I'm not right for you. You need someone who'll...'

'Someone who'll stay?' Anger splashed colour across her cheeks. 'Someone who'll stick around?' She laughed, cold and harsh. 'Surely you don't believe I expected something permanent because of this? I didn't. Especially not from you!'

Her words stung. 'It's not—'

'I have to go.' She snatched her glasses from the dashboard and shoved them onto her face. 'This was a silly mistake. An error in judgement, that was all. The sooner we both forget about it, the better.'

She snatched up her coat and got out of the car. 'Please—don't read too much into this. I woke up in your arms in the darkness and let lust get the better of me, that's all. Any red-blooded woman would have done the same. Would have forgotten herself for a moment.'

'It meant more than that.' It had meant more to Nate, but that wasn't a thought he could examine here and now.

She stepped fully from the car and straightened. 'Let's just agree that it's as well the blackout ended when it did.'

'And you think we'll just forget this happened?' Harsh emotions struggled inside him. He clenched the steering wheel, fighting against—he didn't know exactly what. The need to climb out after her, to drag her back into his arms and make even more of a mess of this? They should forget. It would be best for both of them.

'Now that it's over, it's over.' She shrugged and bent back into the car for just long enough to snatch her bag and the red cushion from the floor, then straightened. 'And I'm going back to what I should have focused on from the beginning. Working hard and praying hard that Henry will hurry up and get better.'

'Of course I'm looking forward to the dinner, Henry. I'm sure it'll be great, as always.' Chrissy had all but forgotten about the annual Montbank dinner, held as a thank-you gesture from Henry to his faithful employees.

She had been too absorbed in other problems to realise the dinner was almost upon them.

After that disaster in the car park days ago, she didn't exactly feel like celebrating. Her hand where it held the phone receiver shook. She gritted her teeth and wished she felt more in control.

The remembrance of what she and Nate had shared refused to leave her. His ultimate rejection still hurt.

'I need to rescue more plants. Maybe I'll start a plant rescue shelter. At least plants appreciate my attention and efforts.' Then again, more of her rescued plants faded away than survived, usually.

'Fine. So not even plants can stand being close to me. So what? They're still good therapy, and one day I'll work out how to make them live.'

Henry cleared his throat noisily into the phone. 'Beg pardon, my dear?'

'Nothing, Henry. It wasn't anything important.'

At her mumbled words, Nate glanced up. She sat at her desk, he at his. From the corner of her eye she could see he was using the phone. Speaking in grim undertones. He had been at it all morning. 'If he draws back any farther, he'll no longer be in the same building. Is this how it's to be from now on?'

Henry made a grumpy noise into the phone. 'Are you listening to me, Chris…Christianna?'

'Sorry. I promise I'll go to the dinner, Henry. You'll be well-represented.' *And every bite will choke me because your grandson will be there, too, and being near him is the last thing I want or need.*

She didn't know how she would get through the remainder of Nate's time here. Working with him, being in constant contact was hard to bear.

'…so if you could just bundle the files into a secure bag and have them couriered to the house for me?'

In the expectant pause, she realised Henry had asked for all the accountancy files he kept in his locked filing cabinet, along with data spreadsheets and computer disks from each department for the current month. 'Are you sure you're up to reviewing all of that? Surely it can wait until you're better—'

'I'm perfectly capable.' He spoke angrily. 'You just do your job and have the ma…materials couriered to me!'

It was the first time Henry had ever snapped at her, and it hurt. 'Of course. I'll see to it straight away.'

'There's a spare key to the filing cabinet in an unmarked pouch in the strongroom on the highest shelf directly to

An Important Message from the Editors

Dear Reader,

Because you've chosen to read one of our fine romance novels, we'd like to say "thank you!" And, as a **special** way to thank you, we've selected <u>two more</u> of the books you love so well **plus** two exciting Mystery Gifts to send you— absolutely <u>FREE</u>!

Please enjoy them with our compliments...

Pam Powers

Lift here

Peel off seal and place inside...

How to validate your Editor's
"Thank You"
FREE GIFTS

1. Peel off gift seal from front cover. Place it in space provided at right. This automatically entitles you to receive 2 FREE BOOKS and 2 FREE mystery gifts.

2. Send back this card and you'll get 2 new Silhouette *Romance®* novels. These books have a cover price of $4.25 or more each in the U.S. and $4.99 or more each in Canada, but they are yours to keep absolutely free.

3. There's no catch. You're under no obligation to buy anything. We charge nothing—ZERO—for your first shipment. And you don't have to make any minimum number of purchases—not even one!

4. The fact is, thousands of readers enjoy receiving their books by mail from The Silhouette Reader Service™. They enjoy the convenience of home delivery...they like getting the best new novels at discount prices BEFORE they're available in stores... and they love their Reader to Reader subscriber newsletter featuring author news, special book offers, book reviews and much more!

5. We hope that after receiving your free books you'll want to remain a subscriber. But the choice is yours— to continue or cancel, any time at all! So why not take us up on our invitation, with no risk of any kind. You'll be glad you did!

GET TWO *Free* MYSTERY GIFTS...

SURPRISE MYSTERY GIFTS COULD BE YOURS **FREE** AS A SPECIAL "THANK YOU" FROM THE EDITORS

DETACH AND MAIL CARD TODAY!

Yes! I have placed my
Editor's "Thank You" seal in the
space provided at right. Please
send me 2 free books and
2 free mystery gifts. I
understand I am under no
obligation to purchase any
books, as explained on the
back and on the opposite page.

PLACE
FREE GIFTS
SEAL
HERE

310 SDL EFX3   210 SDL EFWS

FIRST NAME	LAST NAME

ADDRESS

APT.#	CITY

STATE/PROV.	ZIP/POSTAL CODE

(S-R-10/06)

Thank You!

the left of the door. Make sure you put it back when you're…when you're done.' Although his voice had softened somewhat, Henry hung up abruptly.

When Nate finalised his phone call and left the office with a muttered, 'I'll be back in a minute,' she headed straight for the strongroom and that hidden key.

The last thing she wanted was to be hauling files from Henry's office while Nate sat in it.

Bad enough that she still hummed with awareness from that car-park debacle, drat his muscled biceps and beautifully sculpted chest!

Less than a minute after the courier left, the telephone rang. She dredged deep for the appropriate upbeat, professional tone. 'Chrissy Gable. How may I help you?'

'This is Paul Erickson. I'd like to speak to Nate Barrett, please.' The man had an accent that she couldn't quite place.

'Mr Barrett has stepped out for a minute.' She offered to take a message, and after a momentary hesitation the man gave it to her.

Her usual neat penmanship faltered as she realised the significance of what she was transcribing onto paper. Nevertheless, she recorded the message faithfully. Took her leave politely of the man, assuring him that she would, indeed, ensure that Mr Barrett got the message.

Oh, she would give it to him all right!

Nate returned to the office a few minutes later. 'Is that for me?'

'Yes, actually. It is.' It would have been nice if she had remained in the rather bland, too-angry-to-feel-it-any-more frame of mind that had overcome her.

Unfortunately, when she looked at Nate the numbness left her. Anger swelled, rapidly filling its place. Yielding to the inevitable, she surged to her feet and flung the note at him.

'Your *recruit* apologised for phoning back earlier than arranged, but he wanted to let you know that he has made his decision. He will be delighted to accept the position as the new permanent head of Montbank Shipping Australia.'

Nate glanced at the note, then tucked it casually into his inside suit-jacket pocket.

Casually! How could the man act like that about something so monumental? So appalling? So wrong?

'You've hidden this from me.' *You don't intend to even see your grandfather's illness through. You're going to replace him like some grocery item that's past its expiry date.*

'When were you planning to tell me? The day Henry's replacement arrived? When were you planning to tell Henry? Or did you think he was simply too past it to have a say?'

How could Nate treat his grandfather so casually, with such disregard for Henry's feelings and rights?

Nate's hands clenched. A muscle beneath his jaw tightened. His gaze met and held hers for the first time in days and his eyes softened with...what?

Pity? For her? Did he think she was upset because of him? Because this meant he would be leaving soon?

You are upset, she told herself. *Admit it.*

He eased the clenched hands, but the tension in his face remained. 'I never said I would work in Henry's place forever.'

'No. You just let me believe you would stay through his recovery, and didn't correct me when I made that assumption.' She felt sick. Physically sick with a combination of heartache and disappointment. 'You might as well have lied to me outright. It's that close to the same thing.'

'It isn't.' He took a step toward her. Reached for her arms, then stopped. Dropped his hands. Stepped back again. ' didn't lie to you, Chrissy. And I tried to tell you from the star that Henry couldn't just walk back into this job. You didn't want to hear it.'

How *could* she hear it? Henry was like a surrogate parent. If she lost him as her boss…

More importantly, why *should* she have to hear it? Nate's actions would devastate Henry. She gave Nate the full benefit of every angry, condemning emotion churning inside her.

Turned them all on him through eyes that stung behind the barrier of her glasses. 'He might be your grandfather, but you have no right to try to push Henry out of his position running this company.'

Overwhelmed, heart-sore, fighting the whisper that insisted Henry *did* need to slow down and she had simply been ignoring that knowledge, she swallowed hard. 'Even if Henry had agreed to retire, which he hasn't, why would you choose someone from outside the firm?'

'There's nobody here who qualifies to take over.' For a moment, his gaze seemed to beg her to understand. Then he hardened his expression once more. 'I had to go further afield. I've chosen someone from my—from Montbank's overseas arm.'

'You can't just do that.'

'Be reasonable.' He rammed a hand through his hair. 'Do you think I haven't agonised over this? Do you think the decision came easily to me? My grandfather is no longer fit enough to run this place. I told you before and I say it again now. It's time you accepted that. Henry will have to accept it, too.'

'I'll tell him what you've done.' A desperate feeling swamped her. *He's right. You know he is.* 'That you've hired someone to replace him permanently. He has the right to know what you've been plotting.'

And I don't care if this means you'll be gone any day. I don't!

The mouth that had showed hers such tenderness, such sweetness, firmed and hardened into a determined line. 'There's no need for you to speak to him. *I'll* break it to him. *I'll* convince him he needs to retire, and that Erickson is the man to replace him.'

'When?' She fought to control her raging emotions. 'When will you tell him? When will you leave?'

'I'll tell him soon. Maybe tonight.' The look on his face said it couldn't come soon enough. 'I'll leave as soon as Erickson can get here.'

'You may have helped me once, that first day at the hospital, but you don't really care about your grandfather.' Chrissy drew a deep, shaky breath. 'You never have, but I'll take care of him.'

She would, too, if it took every ounce of determination she possessed. 'I'll be there for him. Just like when the stroke happened. Just like six years ago when he was trying to get over you leaving him.'

'You know I have to go, Chrissy. It's more important now than ever.'

'I don't have time to discuss this.' She snatched up a note from her desk, and grabbed her keys and shoulder bag from her drawer. Knew she was refusing to see the truth, but couldn't face it anyway. 'As it happens, I have a business matter of my own to attend to right now. If I'm lucky, it will keep me out of the office for the rest of the day.'

Nate watched helplessly as Chrissy stalked past him. Her eyes were full of fire, her expression angry and hurt and so damned brave. He wanted to hold her so much that his arms physically ached to be around her. Instead, he was doing his best to leave her.

'Chrissy.' Helplessness swamped him. 'I never intended to cause you pain. Not about Henry. Nor the other morning—'

'Don't worry about me, Nate.' Her chin firmed and she tossed back her head in a show of determined defiance. 'I'll soon get over that incident. After all, there are plenty of other men in the world. Maybe I'll just pick one of them to complete my sexual education!'

CHAPTER NINE

MAYBE I'll just pick one of them. On those words, Chrissy had rushed from the office.

'I can't get her threat out of my mind.' Nate turned the car in the direction of the hideaway cottage and tried not to imagine Chrissy making love with some other guy.

He failed. Just as he had failed each time he thought of it as he waited in vain for her to return to the office this afternoon. And as he drove toward Henry's home to speak with him this evening.

'The conversation with Henry went well, too.' Sarcasm laced his muttered words.

Nate had broached the topic of retirement as gently as he could. Henry had refused to contemplate his suggestion. Had simply given him a stubborn look, thanked him flatly and assured him he would be back in the saddle in no time. That made two people living in fantasy land.

Restless, frustrated with the impasse, his thoughts churning and with no answers in sight, Nate had climbed into his car and simply driven. All over the city. For hours, as he tried to regain his equilibrium.

What really got to him was that it all kept coming back to Chrissy. Didn't matter if he was thinking of work, or his grandfather, or what to eat for dinner.

'You're hooked on her. She never leaves your thoughts.' Somehow, despite his determination to do otherwise, he had allowed feelings for her to grow. Affection? Or something more? Whatever, the feelings were uncomfortable. Alien. Threatening.

He finally stopped outside the cottage, but instead of going inside he restlessly pulled out his cellphone and dialled the number for Chrissy's apartment. If he could just talk to her again. Explain things better so she would understand there was no choice…

'Hello?' A breathless Sophia answered the phone.

'It's Nate Barrett. Is Chrissy there? It's business.' Well, it was business in a sense. The business of saving his sanity. Besides, he should tell Chrissy that Henry had objected to his suggestion of retirement. That should make her as happy as it made him fed-up.

'Oh, sorry, Nate. Chrissy's out with Joe.' Soph drew a hurried breath. 'We're all busy tonight. Bella's out and I'm about to go, too. In fact, I think that's my ride tooting in the street.'

Chrissy. Out. With some other guy.

Maybe I'll just choose one to complete my sexual education.

Even as Nate warned himself that his reaction was irrational, that perhaps he should calm down before he did anything he might regret later, jealousy and fury roared through him.

He had to call on every bit of self-control he owned to speak politely. 'It really is important that I find her, Sophia. Do you know where she went?'

Soph rattled off the address for a popular cabaret venue, then hastily hung up.

Nate pocketed his cellphone and then, jaw clenched, caution gone, he went after Chrissy Gable.

'Thank you, Joe. The cabaret was lovely.' Chrissy smiled at her neighbour and friend, and hoped her smile didn't reflect her misery. 'It was nice of you to invite me.'

'For you, my love, anything. Besides, I probably wouldn't have gone by myself, and I already had the free tickets.' Joe made a show of tucking her arm through his. 'It would have been a shame to waste them.'

They stood on the crowded street outside. The one downside of the cabaret had been that it was way too hot in there. As a result, Joe still had their outdoor coats draped over his arm.

He spotted someone in the crowd, called out, then turned back to her. 'Will you excuse me for just a second? That's Enrico. I'd like to say hello….'

'Sure. I'll wait here.' Her gaze followed Joe for a moment, then she turned away.

Moments later, a man materialised at her side. He wore rough work clothes, with a woollen cap pulled low over his eyes. 'I've been watching you, Chrissy Gable, and now it's time to warn you.'

'Warn me about what? How do you know my name?' With no sign of Joe near by, she began to edge away from the man. 'I'm here with a friend. Please go away.'

'Tell Nate Barrett to keep his nose away from the docks.' The man shoved his face close to hers. 'If he doesn't call off his investigation team, he might just find himself at the bottom of the ocean somewhere. With rocks in his pockets. *Capisce*?'

'Who are you?' She tried not to sound as rattled as she felt. 'You can't just go around making threats.'

But the man had melted away into the crowd.

Chrissy stood frozen, shaken to the core. What had the man meant? Why would he threaten Nate?

'Well, that was nice—' Joe's cheerful voice stopped mid-sentence. He quickly wrapped his free arm around her. 'What's happened? You look terrified.'

'It was nothing.' She didn't know why she chose not to tell Joe. Actually, she did. She wanted to tell *Nate*. To warn him.

She needed to hear his reassurance that all would be well. That the man had been some lunatic and Nate was perfectly safe and would stay that way.

'Did you team up with your friend, Joe?' She lifted herself up on high heels and dropped a kiss on his cheek. 'I enjoyed our night, but I understand if you want to go on somewhere else now without me. In truth, I've had enough, anyway.'

I'd like you to go, so I can focus on what just happened, and how to deal with it.

'Then I'll see you into a taxi.' He hugged her close, and whispered, 'You look way too hot in that dress. If I leave you alone, you'll have to fight off a mob of admirers. On the other hand,' he added wickedly, 'I could be tempted to steal the dress for myself.'

Despite herself, she laughed. 'You might keep trying to steal Gertie, but you know you don't cross-dress.'

'Well, no, but it got a smile out of you.' Joe grinned, and his gaze softened. 'Life is never as painful if you can laugh at it a little. That's my motto.'

'It's a smart motto.' But her emotions were too raw right now for her to adhere to it as well as she wished she could.

The heartache of Nate's rejection was enough. Worry about him pushed her emotions over the edge. Despite her effort to hold them back, tears smarted against her eyelids. Two stinging, hot drops spilled over.

'Hey, now.' Joe pulled a face, and wiped the tears from beneath her eyes with his fingertips. 'Tell you what. Let's go back to my place. We can make cocoa and talk. I can cancel my other arrangements.'

'Thanks, Joe, but I'll pass on the cocoa this time. I think I just want to be alone.' She leaned into his hug. Wrapped her arms around his middle, and pressed her face against his silk shirt. 'You're the best, though. I've decided you can have my share of Gertie when I die.'

'Gee, thanks.' He gave her a squeeze back. 'If you're sure you don't want me to stick around?'

She nodded.

'Then I guess I'd best get going. Let's get you that taxi, all right?'

'Sure.' She mumbled it into his chest and wondered why it was that only Nate's chest made her want to explode with longing.

Well, Joe didn't really count. And she hadn't exactly tried out any other men since she told Nate she reciprocated his attitude and didn't want him, either.

It wouldn't matter how many chests you snuggled up to. You only want Nate. At least be honest enough to admit it.

'Do you know, Joe?' She mumbled into his shirt. 'Honesty sucks. Especially when you're being honest with yourself.'

'How touching. I'm relieved to see you aren't letting the grass grow under your feet, Christianna.' The arctic voice brought her head up.

Nate. Safe. Furious. Here in front of her right now. But not hers. Never hers. Her heart cried against that knowledge.

Tears smarted again. She swallowed them down and looked around her, half-afraid that someone would leap from the crowd and attack Nate this instant.

Joe dropped his arm, and she stepped away. 'Nate, what are you doing here?'

'We have to talk.' His grating tone, the look in his eyes and the tightness of his facial muscles finally penetrated beyond her fear.

He was jealous. Even as hope soared, she reminded herself it wasn't exactly complimentary that Nate assumed she had walked straight out of his arms into someone else's. Forget hoping, anyway. She mustn't let her heart go off on any more self-defeating tangents.

Joe took a step forward, the muscles honed from working on cars tensed beneath his clothes. 'I don't like the tone you just used with my friend.'

Chrissy wasn't sure Nate even heard.

Instead, his gaze raked her from head to foot, taking in the clingy silver gown with the keyhole cut that revealed her navel. Finally his gaze came to rest on her eyes—*sans* glasses, because Joe knew they were mostly for show and had begged her not to wear them.

The chilly air made itself belatedly known, and she shivered and hugged her arms around her middle.

For a moment she thought dark desire flared in Nate's eyes, but then he simply looked angry again. 'I'll take you home.'

In other circumstances, she would have refused. After all, she *was* out with someone else, even if that someone was only a friend.

Nate didn't know that, yet he acted as though he had the right to come and haul her away like some protective parent or something.

One thing stopped her from venting her spleen at him. She had to tell him what had just happened. 'Yes. Let's go.' The grittiness of her tone couldn't be helped. That was what happened when anger and heartache and a dozen other emotions warred inside a person. 'I need to talk to you, too.'

She turned to Joe. Tried to smile. 'This is important, Joe. You go on.'

Joe hesitated, looking from one to the other of them, then eventually nodded. He handed her coat to her and walked away.

Then it was just her and Nate, and she wanted him away from

this crowded place where threat had come so swiftly and silently. She wanted him, period, but that was a separate heartache.

'Put your coat on before you freeze to death.' On that grumpy instruction, Nate plucked the coat from her hands and held it open.

After a slight hesitation, she slipped her arms into the sleeves. It would be pointless to catch a chill just because Nate sounded cross and bossy. One of them behaving in a juvenile manner was enough!

Then Nate closed his eyes and breathed deeply as they stood close together, and she forgave him for his grumpiness. Didn't she want to be near him just as much? Even after the harsh words that had passed between them.

I don't want to be your enemy, Nate, but I don't believe I can be only your friend, either.

He clamped his jaw and stepped back. 'Sorry. It's difficult for me to be near you….' He trailed to a stop as though only just realising what he had said. Cleared his throat. 'The car's this way.'

If he hadn't breathed her in as though he had been starved for her and admitted his need for her, she might have been able to hold out.

Instead, her defences began to crack. She had no control over the reaction whatsoever.

When they climbed into his car and he began the journey toward her apartment, she struggled to break the silence. But words stuck in her throat. She wasn't sure she could speak rationally, without those cracks in her defences breaking her completely apart.

He still doesn't want you. Not permanently. And a fling was not enough. She acknowledged that now.

They stopped outside her home. She finally spoke. 'Someone threatened you…'

'What's going on, Chrissy? I find you with some guy and you're scared out of your wits.' Confusion and leashed anger warred in his tone. 'A part of me wants to pulverise him on your behalf, but something else is warning me if I did that, I'd be making a mistake.'

'You would be. Joe's a neighbour and a *friend*.'

'*More* than a friend?' His tone was silky. Soft. Yet she sensed the steel beneath.

'A very good platonic friend. I've known him since I was in high school. He had nothing to do with what scared me.'

'Are you telling me the truth?' Nate stopped. Shook his head. Started again. 'If it wasn't your *friend* Joe who frightened you, then what happened?'

'Joe excused himself for a moment after the show.' She forced back a shudder. 'While I was waiting for him, a man came up to me. He knew me by name and told me to make sure you keep your nose out of things at the docks otherwise you might end up…dead.'

She hated to even say the word. How could she bear it if something happened to Nate? 'I don't know what's going on, but you have to promise me you'll stay away from the docks. Don't ever go there.'

'It must be the investigation.' He growled the words out, then swore fluently. 'We must be close to figuring out what's going on.'

'Who must be? What are you talking about?' She wanted his assurance that he would keep safe. She wanted to shake him, damn it, then hold him close and make him promise to be OK.

So much for forgetting him and getting on with her life— even if he *was* still working with her on a daily basis!

'Those phone discussions with the head of our stevedore company…' He seemed to hesitate, then sighed and went on. 'The stevedore—Rick Johnson—has picked up oddities in some of our dealings with his company. Although very minor, those things have added up enough to raise his suspicions.'

'And you decided to investigate on the strength of that?' She didn't mean to sound disbelieving, but it seemed overly cautious. 'What if it's just his imagination?'

'As well as the stevedore's concerns, I've discovered accounting discrepancies within Montbank's.' His frustration coloured his tone. 'It's fair to assume the two things could be linked. That's the reason for putting investigators on to the situation at the docks, as well.'

'And within the office? Where exactly have you discovered these problems?'

Nate was silent for a long moment. When he spoke his tone was restrained, almost apologetic. 'The problems appear to be generating from within Henry's offices.'

'But that would mean…' It would mean that either she or Henry were committing crimes against the company.

Obviously Henry wouldn't sabotage his own company. That left her, and suddenly the night she had taken Henry's crossword puzzle home came back to her in clear, sharp detail. 'You thought I—'

'No.' His denial was loud in the stillness of the car's interior. He lowered his voice. 'No. I needed an explanation for something that looked odd. You gave it. End of story.'

She searched his face. Believed him, but still needed answers. 'Then what's happening? Why is all this going on?'

I'm scared, Nate. I'm scared for your safety.

He reached for her, tugged her around until she faced him then searched her eyes with a narrowed gaze. 'Whatever's going on, I intend to get to the bottom of it. Tell me everything you can about the man who spoke to you tonight. Maybe there's a clue there somewhere.'

She recounted the warning as exactly as she could remember it. Described the man as best she could. It wasn't enough. She knew it, but it was all she had to offer. 'What will you do about this? Watching your back isn't going to be enough, is it?'

'It might have been an empty threat.' Nate said it, but didn't for a moment believe it. Someone had tracked Chrissy down to give her that warning. Why bother, if they meant no harm?

'Aside from your escort, who knew where you were going tonight?'

'Nobody. It was a last-minute thing. I bumped into Joe, he had tickets to a cabaret and nobody to go with. Bella was out. Soph had her head in the kitchen sink performing some sort of hair art I don't really want to think about.' Her eyes widened. 'You don't think they're in danger, too, do you? That man knew who I was.'

Nate watched the realisation crash over her that there was only one way the man had known where to find her tonight. 'He followed me. He followed me from here!'

'It's the most likely answer.' And what Nate wanted to do, in truth, was gather Chrissy and her sisters and take them all somewhere safe until he'd sorted this out. 'The threat was given to you, but it was against me.

'If I back off with things at the docks, or at least make it look as though I have, you should be safe. I don't think they'd care less about your sisters. But I won't take any chances, Chrissy, and you mustn't either.'

Keeping her safe was the only thing that mattered. 'I'll take you up to the apartment. If your sisters are home, I want to talk to them, too. If not, I'll stay until they get there.'

'Yes.' She gave a delicate shudder and reached for the door handle. 'Let's go up. Quickly.'

Hustling her up the stairs to her apartment was an excuse

to wrap his arm around her back, to tug her against his side where he wanted her to be.

The apartment was silent, just a single lamp burning on an end table beside the sofa.

'I'll check the bedrooms,' Chrissy whispered, 'but I can tell they're not home.'

When she headed for the small hallway, Nate was before her. 'Why don't I check, first?'

Why don't you remain in the living area, where I know you're safe from possible harm?

Her hand rose to grip the back of his coat at the waist. He could feel her body heat as she pressed close behind him.

Her voice dropped to a lower whisper. 'We'll go together.'

They checked the small bathroom, then a room that, by the array of exotic-looking clothing strewn around, had to be Bella's.

Next came the second bedroom. It was larger, and was clearly shared by Chrissy and Sophia. The room was empty. The apartment was secure.

Nate's gaze honed in immediately on the arty prints on the left-hand wall. The chimes dangling from the ceiling.

Then moved to the bed nearest those things. His jaw locked. Words forced themselves through lips that did their best to keep them in, and failed. 'This is your bed?'

He spotted a row of indoor plants in varying degrees of demise in a planter on the window sill and suppressed a smile. Why didn't she simply give up trying?

Because then she wouldn't be Chrissy.

'Yes.' She cleared her throat, her gaze darting anywhere but at him. 'Um. Soph and I share. Neither of us snore, or, um, or anything.'

Her blush was beautiful. If he didn't want her so much, he might tempt fate and try to steal a kiss. He settled for a smile as he watched her fidget.

'I'll get us some coffee or something.' Before he could stop her she had unbuttoned the coat, slid out of it and dropped it carelessly onto the bed.

The dress had blind-sided him the first time. When he saw her in Joe's arms, wearing the slinky outfit, desire and jealousy had almost struck him down. *The guy is a friend. Just that.*

Now all Nate wanted to do was look at her. Then take the dress off her so he could enjoy the pure perfection of her without any adornment at all.

He clenched his fists, but when she turned to the door his arm snaked out. Gripped the soft flesh of her upper arm. It was a small step from there to tug her against his chest. He didn't do it, but with a sigh he cupped the back of her neck.

Such a delicate neck, fine-boned and slender. 'Tell me that dress is borrowed from one of your sisters and I'll never see you in it again.'

'You don't like it?' She drew back against his hold. Seemed as though his opinion of the dress might actually matter to her.

And he, fool that he was, raised his gaze and let it lock with hers so she could see for herself what he thought of her dress. 'I like it. Enough that I want to stroke my fingers over it and feel the way it moulds to your shape.' His tone deepened. 'Enough to take it off you if I'm still looking at it ten seconds from now.'

'We decided...' Her lips mouthed resistance. The fire in her eyes belied it.

'Yeah. We did.' Right now he wasn't quite sure why they had decided to stay away from each other. But the tense, wary expression in her eyes helped him to back off. She was confused right now. So was he. And they had other things to worry about. Now wasn't the right time for this. 'I'll start the coffee while you change clothes.'

She closed the bedroom door after him. When she joined

him minutes later, she had pulled on dark green trousers and a fluffy matching jumper, both of which hugged her like a second skin.

'At least you'll be warm.' His muttered words earned him a raised eyebrow before she fell on the coffee, wrapping both hands around the mug while she inhaled the fragrance.

'I see you found the coffee plunger.'

'Yeah.' He took a draught of his own drink, but his mind was elsewhere. Several elsewheres, actually, and that was not a good thing. They had a problem, and they needed to focus on it alone.

She seemed to realise it, too, and lowered her mug from her mouth, before gesturing to her left. 'Let's go into the living room. I'd like to ask you some questions, now that I've had a moment to get my bearings.'

She headed for one of the roomy wing chairs. Nate settled on the sofa and tried not to think of kissing her.

'Will you contact the police? Remove your investigators from the docks?' After another swallow of coffee, she set the mug on the low table and focused her attention very directly on him. 'How do we handle this to make sure everyone stays safe, whilst ensuring we still get to the bottom of what's happening?'

They were his questions, too, and the answers were limited. 'I've left messages for both investigators to call me urgently. I want them off the docks investigation.'

'That's good. It will protect them.' She bobbed her head in approval.

He could only be grateful that her hair was still firmly secured on her head. If she had let it down when she'd changed clothes, he doubted his self-restraint would have made it past *Here's your coffee*. 'I'll let Rick Johnson know what's happened, and that the investigators won't be back.'

'What happens then?' She tucked one leg under her in the

comfy chair, leaned both arms on the padded side and set her chin on her hands. Her gaze was direct. Trusting. Confident that he would have the right answers. 'It's all the more important now for us to find out what's going on. You won't really be safe until we do.'

He wouldn't be safe? What about her? Her concern for his safety moved him. He set his cup down with extra care, and told himself it was not necessary to lift her from the chair into his arms, stride the length of that small hallway and love her in that girlish bed until they were both senseless. 'I'm more concerned about keeping *you* safe.'

'Why did you turn up tonight? Outside the cabaret?' Her brows knitted. 'It wasn't a coincidence, was it? You sought me out. How? Why?'

'I went to see Henry tonight.' *Your sister told me you were out on a date and I wanted to pulverise that date, so I simply went after you.* 'Henry's happy to be at home, looks like hell and is upset that Margaret's taken off again.'

She didn't speak. Just waited.

He went on. 'I wanted to tell you that I broached the topic of replacing him permanently.'

The look of tenderness changed to one of remembered irritation. 'I don't know why you keep insisting—'

'Yes, you do.' He climbed from his chair. Faced her across the small expanse of living room until she, too, got to her feet.

She glared at him.

Ah, Chrissy. Accept it. 'You do know why I keep insisting. Henry either slows up and has a hope of maintaining some sort of quality of life, or he goes back to heading up the company full-time in the same active role, and three, six, twelve months later we could well be planning his funeral instead of his retirement.'

The harsh words made her face pale. Then her mouth

trembled. She bit her lip and for long, long moments her gaze searched his. A sigh poured from her. An aching, reluctant sound of acceptance that gave him no pleasure whatsoever. 'I've been in denial.'

'You just wanted him to be able to be his old self.' Nate wanted it, too. Wanted a way out from all the complications inherent in what had happened to Henry.

He wanted his grandfather to be happy, and didn't know how to make that possible. 'I shouldn't have talked to him yet. It could have waited. I should have held off until I had a better plan about approaching him.'

'How did Henry take it?' She took a step toward him.

'He told me he would be back at work in no time and refused to discuss it further.'

She winced. 'Is he all right? He didn't get too upset?'

'Nothing to set his blood pressure off or anything.' His lips formed a wry line. 'I think I'm still recovering, though.'

'I'm sorry I refused to see the need for this sooner.' She shook her head. 'It will be the end of an era when he stops working there. That scares me. Montbank Shipping is all I've known since I left school, and Henry's been…kind to me.'

'Don't blame yourself for not wanting it to end.' Nate certainly didn't blame her. How could he blame her for anything? She had been there for Henry while he was on the other side of the world, telling himself he was happy moving around, never putting down roots.

That old life didn't look so appealing now.

'Careful.' She injected a playful note into her tone and reached for his hands in a chummy sort of gesture. 'If you don't watch it, you'll end up being all nice and sweet and stuff.'

'We can't have that.' He drawled the words, but his attention was on their clasped hands. What had started as a simple, friendly gesture turned immediately to something more.

And it felt so right. So damned right to connect with her in a world that was all going wrong. He looked into the lovely eyes that were all his to see, because she hadn't replaced her glasses since she got here.

Did she realise she had failed to put them on? To put up that flimsy barrier that seemed to mean so much to her? 'Chrissy, I—'

'Henry loves you.' She squeezed his hands, her face as open and generous as her words. 'He'll come to understand that you're only trying to act in his best interests. He won't resent you once he realises this is best for him.'

Was she so keen to see him go, then? But the sadness in the backs of her eyes told him she was being brave for Henry's sake. Was trying to accept what had to be done.

I don't want to leave you. He stopped the thought before it could find voice.

'Things have been difficult since he remarried.'

'Yes.' She half smiled, then shook her head. 'What really went on, Nate? Between you and Margaret? I don't mean that I think you had an affair, but what—?'

'I've never spoken of it.' He hesitated, then his mouth firmed with decision. 'But I want you to know. I don't want you to go on thinking—'

'If it's too personal—'

'It is personal, particularly to Henry, but I know I can trust you with it. I'd been away on vacation. I met Margaret for the first time at the wedding reception.' His mouth twisted in memory of what had at first seemed to be some sort of misconception on his part. Maybe Margaret was just really friendly and he was reading into it or something? 'Margaret started stalking me there, wouldn't leave me alone.

'They didn't have a honeymoon. I wanted to move out of the house, but it's a big place. Henry wanted me to stay and

I figured I could keep out of their way for a few days until I found an apartment. It all happened very suddenly.'

'Nate, I'm sorry. I shouldn't have asked.' She fidgeted with her hands.

'I'm glad you did.' He realised it was true. 'When I realised Margaret wasn't just fooling around or being overly friendly with her overtures toward me, I told her to back off.' His mouth tightened. 'There was no way she could have misunderstood, yet less than twenty-four hours later I found her waiting naked in my bed. I left. I didn't want Henry to know what she'd done.'

'Why didn't you tell me?' She seemed almost hurt. 'Earlier, when I accused you, you could have told me what really happened.'

'Like you told me about the crossword? Protecting Henry from the truth had become too much of a habit. But I don't want you to go on thinking I simply walked away from him on a whim.' He groaned in frustration, turned his back on her to gaze sightlessly into the tiny kitchenette.

'I left to protect him. My staying there was unhealthy for him. I had to leave so he could have his chance. He wanted Margaret. I don't know why, but he did.'

She stepped forward. Touched the back of his hand with slender fingers for just a moment. 'Thank you for telling me. I resented you for so long, and that was wrong of me. I'm...I'm sorry. And...I understand now. When will you leave?'

'I won't leave until I know you're safe from harm.' He didn't want to go at all. 'About us—'

'Nate.' She cut him off. 'There is no us. We just both have to remember that until you're gone.'

Footsteps sounded outside and Bella's familiar series of knocks rapped on the door.

Chrissy got to her feet. 'That's my sister. I'll explain things. There's no need for you to stay any longer.'

CHAPTER TEN

'IT SEEMS our precautions have worked.' A week had passed since the threat to Nate's safety. Now they were celebrating the passing of another year for Montbank Shipping. Chrissy wanted to celebrate, but it would be easier if she wasn't so aware of the man at her side. She swallowed hard. 'I think everything might be OK now. That there won't be any further threat to the company.'

To your safety.

'Let's hope so.' Nate lifted the bottle of chardonnay and refilled their glasses. 'Here's to that hope.'

For a moment, she caught a glimpse of fire in his eyes. Then he lowered his gaze, and clinked his glass to hers.

Had she imagined it? Before she could decide, Nate turned to the others seated at their table. Lifted his glass and raised his voice. 'To Montbank's, and to all of you.'

A round of hear-hears echoed as people touched glasses. It was a good night, or at least—it was good to feel safe after living on edge for days. Good to feel that Nate was safe. She just wished she didn't yearn for him so. Didn't crave him in a way she couldn't seem to control, despite reminding herself that a relationship between them wouldn't work.

He hadn't changed. Neither had she. She lowered her gaze

to her plate and toyed with the napkin in her lap. At least things really did seem to be better on the work front, although Henry still wouldn't talk about being replaced.

Nate had enlisted the help of the stevedore's leader in seeking some answers at the docks without raising further suspicion. He had also asked the investigators to examine the records at Montbank's itself, and Chrissy had done all she could to accommodate them.

She should have been pleased, but was beginning to wonder if it was a mistake to push Nate away. Why not take what she could get on his terms? Even if those terms were so much less than she might choose. Her heart longed for something…

'Why so pensive?' His hand touched hers where it rested in her lap. He drew back just quickly enough to make her wonder if the touch had seared his senses as it had hers. 'We've done what we can. Hopefully our stevedore will come through with some answers eventually.'

'Hopefully, yes.' Her pulse accelerated in reaction to his touch. Awareness held her fast, but so, too, did uncertainty.

What was he thinking and feeling right now? 'That is a good thing, and we'll work out what's going on with our Montbank accounting.'

She did her best to converse easily while her thoughts churned. At least they would probably resolve their work issues. Eventually. Recalling her visit to Henry earlier tonight, she sighed. 'Henry still has those files I couriered to him, though. I did ask again, but he was a bit cranky.'

'I'll collect the files the next time I'm over there. At least, I'll try to diplomatically do that.' His low tone was too intimate for her comfort. He leaned closer to her and her heart stumbled. Then he gestured toward her plate, as though nothing had happened. 'How's your meal?'

'Nice.' She suppressed a sigh, dipped another piece of baby broccoli in the lemon sauce and popped it into her mouth. *I want you so much, Nate, and I want to know if you're feeling the same way.*

His gaze followed the movement of her throat as she chewed and swallowed. 'I, ah…' He cleared his throat, then gestured toward her. 'Where did you get the dress? It's…rather revealing, don't you think?'

'Bella made the dress for me.' It wasn't too revealing. A shiver of pleasure passed through her at the knowledge that Nate couldn't view her outfit rationally. 'It's perfect for evening wear.'

The dress was filmy but not flimsy. Attractive, but not obvious. It made the most of her figure, and was flattering in all the right places.

'What it is, is perfectly alluring.' He growled the words beneath his breath in an accusatory rumble that raised goose-pimples all over her.

And you're perfectly alluring to me, Nate Barrett, and I'm not sure I want to fight that feeling any longer.

He stabbed a sliver of salmon with his fork. Grated the words, 'The fish is good.' Shifted his glare to the wine before them. 'And they've done a good job matching the chardonnay.'

Need bubbled inside her, just waiting….

'The, ah, the salmon *is* good.' She would rather be nibbling Nate's mouth. Sipping from Nate's lips. 'And I like a good chardonnay.'

His fork clattered onto his plate, and fierce blue eyes locked on her. 'If you put into words what your expression tells me you're thinking, I won't be responsible for what follows.'

What if she didn't want him to be responsible?

'We've been good all week.' It was a declaration and a plea. She didn't know if she wanted reassurance, or permission to break out. 'We've managed ourselves,' she whispered. 'Right?'

He touched one of the ringlet curls that Soph had styled to cascade over her shoulders in sassy ripples, and said roughly, 'Let's go mingle. Show our appreciation to these stalwart Montbank folks.'

His silence on the topic told the truth. They had managed because they had buried themselves in business, never delving beneath the surface. If she revealed her willingness, would Nate act on the awareness they shared? Or would he push her away, as he had the last time?

You would be a fool to risk the hurt.

They moved to the first table together, chatted a few moments, but her skin tingled and she struggled to focus on anything but Nate's presence at her side. All the while she told herself she would resist him, because she didn't want that hurt twice over.

Then they drifted apart and spent the next hour catching up with people separately. She didn't want to be away from him, and that reaction scared her, too. Eventually, dessert was served.

Chrissy even managed to return to their table and swallow half her almond cream pastry before she glanced at Nate and lost her appetite. Because every bite he took of his dessert made her think of his mouth on hers.

Heat exploded through her. She sat there and fought with herself, and then Nate got to his feet and held out his hand, a crooked, funny, almost tortured expression on his face. She joined him automatically, but her gaze questioned him.

'The music has started.' His hand tightened on hers as he turned toward the small dance floor at the end of the room. 'It's traditional for the boss to begin the dancing.'

Yes. Henry had indeed made that a tradition, but, 'Henry danced with his wife. Not his PA.'

'I don't have a wife.' He drew her into the centre of the floor, and into his arms.

Her wariness gave way beneath his touch. When she looked into his eyes, she knew he shared her torment.

Someone cut in. She wanted to tell the person to leave them be. To let them stay together this way forever. Nate relinquished her, but the heat in his eyes belied his urbane smile.

Dance after dance passed, and then she found herself facing him again just as a slow, sensual ballad began.

Chrissy drew in her breath. She wanted his arms around her but wasn't sure she could trust herself not to reveal how much she longed for him... She shook her head. 'Oh, no. I don't think it would be a good idea—'

'Probably not.' He drew a shallow breath. 'But just for tonight. Just this. Just one dance. Please.'

Instead of resisting, she stepped into his arms. Her hands came to rest against his chest as they swayed to the music. 'How can we dance so well together when we've never done it before tonight?'

'I don't know.' His hands tightened where he held her. Dark eyelashes lowered over deep, aware blue eyes. 'We fit together.'

'Yes.' She didn't say more. Didn't trust herself to. Instead, her lips parted on a sigh.

His arms tightened. 'Maybe not such a good idea to use that word around me,' he growled, and brought her even closer.

'Nate?' Her arms found their way to his neck. Tightened around him.

'We're safe.' He cupped the curve of her hip with one strong, warm hand. The other moved to the dip of her spine and pressed gently. 'A room full of people. How can we not be safe?'

How, indeed? Why, then, did she feel absolutely unsafe? 'This is simply a reward for getting things under control this week.' Her chin lifted. 'Just that.'

His gaze was too sober, the touch of his hands on her possessive whether he meant it to be or not. He didn't reply.

With a sigh, she relaxed against him anyway. Sultry awareness tugged at chains deep inside her, tried to wrest them from tenuous moorings.

But it was OK. She could keep it under control as she had done all through the week. She would take only this much.

His hold on her tightened. 'Remind me we're not alone, because I can't seem to remember it well enough on my own.' His harsh whisper grazed her earlobe, the side of her neck.

Nate thought she had a better chance of controlling this than he did? Ha, ha. She dared to look at his face, and moaned softly. She didn't want to remind him of any such thing. 'I don't see any other people. I only see you.'

'Chrissy. Sweet…' His mouth was halfway to hers when she became aware that the music had stopped. Had ended long enough ago that they were beginning to draw attention.

Nate realised it, too, and swore softly beneath his breath as he dropped his arms and stepped back. She stumbled back, too, shaken. What to do now? How to tamp down the fire inside?

'I'm, ah…' she flicked an uncoordinated hand to indicate others returning to their tables '…I'm going to speak with a few more people.'

Her gaze shifted to the left and she told him, because she couldn't think of any polite phrases or nice words, 'You go that way.'

'I don't want to walk away, Chrissy. I'm certain you don't want to, either, so maybe we should talk to each other. Should face up to this thing instead of dancing around it any longer.'

She tried for a smile. Failed. Felt her heart race at the possibilities—and at the chance of so much hurt if they talked and he pushed her away once and for all.

I want you, Nate, but I'm afraid to reach out and get hurt. 'Pun intended?'

His mouth softened, but determination shone in his eyes. Hardened the planes of his face. 'You know we can't go on this way.'

Oh, she was tempted. So, so tempted to say yes, let's talk. But what would talking achieve?

I'm scared, Nate. Too scared to talk this out. I'm scared I'll say things you won't want to hear. Monumental things I don't even want to acknowledge are lurking in my heart.

'I can't do this now.' A sense of panic flooded her. 'I just…I can't.'

On those words, she hurried away. From the corner of her eye she saw his harsh face, and the rare indecision before he squared his shoulders, locked it all down and attached himself to a group of guests.

She did the same—on the opposite side of the room. Somehow she got through. She mingled and chatted and laughed until her jaws ached with the effort and she wondered if everyone could sense the brittleness of her gaiety.

Nate kept away from her, but she felt his gaze. Felt it almost as a physical brand. This night needed to be over.

'Will you excuse me?' She smiled at the group of people and moved away. She would thank the kitchen staff, then leave. They had yet to bring out the coffee and twice-baked biscotti, but she couldn't wait any longer.

Delicious scents of pine nut and orange rind, of chocolate and cardamom filled the air. At another time, she would have delighted in those smells.

Her hand was on the swing door when Nate spoke from a little way behind her. 'I guess we had the same idea.'

'To say thanks, then run for the hills?' Chrissy tried to smile as she looked over her shoulder and pushed the swing door open. Tried to look as though she felt cool inside. That she was rational, restrained and in control of herself, instead of the rampaging mess she really was. Just looking at him hurt. At the same time, she couldn't bear the thought of not seeing him every day. Of not being able to look at him any time she wanted to. Any time she needed to.

Because she loved him.

The knowledge locked her feet to the floor. Filled her with a sense of desperation and absolute awe that almost tore her apart. She had fallen in love with Nate.

Had known it even before now, but had refused to acknowledge it. Dear God, what did she do now? She couldn't let Nate know. Couldn't allow him to see what she had just realised.

'Chrissy?' Whatever he saw in her expression, it was enough to make him reach for her. The shutters dropped away and raw hunger etched his face. Emotion pooled in his gaze.

But what emotion, damn it? What was he thinking?

She stopped herself before she begged in her heart for that emotion to be love. Her parents had taught her that no amount of internal hoping or bargaining or wishing or pleading could make someone love her. Now above all other times, she needed to remember that lesson and be strong.

Nate would never love her. He wasn't a man who would give that to her.

For a moment, she thought the roar was the sound of her heart screaming inside her. Then there was a shout from the kitchen. A look of horror wiped all else from Nate's face.

A hoarse cry came from his lips as he grabbed her. Tugged her sharply forward. At the same time, something hot and furious blasted them from behind. His arms clamped around her and he flung them to the floor.

They crashed across it and pain scraped across her shoulder, her elbow. His low grunt revealed he hadn't gone unscathed, either. She lay stunned in his arms, her mind struggling to assimilate what had happened.

An explosion in the kitchen. The kitchen staff. Oh, God, please let them be all right.

Shouts broke out. Dishes clattered. Someone moaned.

Her mouth seemed disconnected from her mind. She struggled to get the words out. 'We have to help them.'

'We will.' Nate pulled her to her feet, tugged her further from the furore, from the heat. 'First, what hurts? Can you see me properly? Show me your back. Let me see if it got you.'

His face was as ashen as she felt. But she didn't feel burnt. 'I'm OK. Are you?'

He nodded.

She gripped his arm. 'We have to—'

'Get help.' He already had his cellphone out, but sirens outside the building made it clear that help was on the way. He put the phone back in his pocket, and turned her gently. Shaking hands patted over her hair and back, then turned her to face him again. 'If your dress or hair had caught fire—'

'They didn't.' Later she could face that possibility and react to it. 'We have to help these people.' They moved together toward the kitchen.

People from the dining room rushed to the scene. Nate shouted them to a standstill. He turned to her. 'Wait here. Stay away from the danger.'

'No. I'm coming with you.' But arms wrapped around her. Female voices soothed.

She struggled to make them understand. She didn't want to be soothed. Nate couldn't go in there without her. She needed to be at his side.

Words crowded at her. Fragments from all around.

'Gas explosion…'

'…oven must have been faulty.'

'Nobody right near it, thank God.'

She broke free at last and moved into the kitchen on legs that wobbled and threatened to drop her onto the floor again. A dozen or so people. Several nursing injuries. Two slumped in chairs. But all conscious.

And Nate in the middle. He took the powder fire extinguisher from the head chef's shaking hands and trained it on the smouldering oven and surrounds.

Her beloved Nate. If fate had taken him from her, how would she have survived? Something inside her coalesced in that moment.

Nate had hinted that they needed to reassess their relationship. Well, she just had, and she was going to have everything she could get with him, even if it was only a night.

Life was too short. So she would find some way to deal with letting go when it ended. When this was over…

'Is it safe? Do we need to get them out?' Her voice sounded odd in her ears.

Nate turned. 'You shouldn't be here.'

'You are.'

A voice intruded. 'Out of the way, please, people. Let's take care of these folks.'

In moments, the kitchen was cleared, people eased onto stretchers or assisted outside to be taken to the nearest Accident and Emergency.

The restaurant owner talked to the police in low tones, sweat beading on his brow. At Nate's request, the crowd dissipated, moved back to the dining area to collect their things and go home.

It wasn't the end to the evening that any of them could have anticipated. Again, Chrissy began to shake as she thought of all that could have happened. If the explosion had been worse. If other things had caught fire.

And then Nate's arms were around her again, and nothing had ever felt so good. She sighed against his chest, pressed her hand over his heart and absorbed the strong, steady beat of it. 'Will they all be OK?'

'Yes.' His mouth pressed against her temple. 'Shock, some minor burns, but nothing worse. The owner will make sure his staff are taken care of. Right now, I'm more concerned about you.'

'It's silly. I just took a tumble across the floor. I don't know why I feel so shaken.' It was a lie. She was shaken because she had discovered she loved him, and realised how it would feel if fate took him from her before she had a chance to show him what he meant to her.

I will show you Nate, even though I know you'll leave.

'You need to go to the hospital, too, my darling.' His gentle words covered her in warmth against the deep chill that had invaded her body. The tightening of his arms around her revealed that strong feelings still lurked.

Her heart swelled in unsolicited hope, because how could he call her his darling if he didn't feel something for her, too? How could he hold her so tightly, if he didn't crave her?

Affection. He feels a degree of affection. It's not the same as love.

'I don't want to go to the hospital. I just… Can we just leave?'

He looked deep in her eyes, then hustled her outside, his jaw clenched. 'I'm not sure you realise how much I want—' A harsh sound came from his throat. 'I'll take you back to the cottage. Attend to those scrapes.'

Before she could agree or disagree, he had bundled her into his car. They were almost at the cottage when he spoke again.

'I can't let you go back to your place, Chrissy. Not right now. Not even into the competent care of your sisters.'

'They're not there. Soph's spending the weekend in the country, and Bella's got some important thing on in Sydney.'

'You shouldn't have told me that.' He stopped the car outside the cottage. In moments, he was at her door. 'Come inside.'

Just that. Two simple words, but her heart raced, hope and need soared. She struggled to contain it, but her hand shook as she placed it in his.

Inside, Nate raised the heat on the electric wall unit. 'It will warm up more in a few minutes.' Instead of moving further into the cottage, he seemed to be locked in position just inside the door. His gaze held hers with such sensual heat that she thought she might melt.

'I'm—not cold.' *I'm burning up with heat for you.*

The planes of his face tightened. 'I'll get something to treat your wounds.'

He turned. Her Nate. Determined to do the right thing.

She looked at him, begged with her eyes for him to stay with her. To make love with her. She didn't know who reached out, but in seconds she was in his arms.

'Dear God, Chrissy.' He pulled her closer still.

And his mouth covered hers.

CHAPTER ELEVEN

NATE's whole body shuddered as he held Chrissy. Kissed her because he needed to have his mouth on hers. To assure himself she was well. Safe. He had contributed to her pain. Had caused some of it. He murmured against her lips, 'I'm sorry I harmed you.'

Sooner or later, you hurt the ones you love. It's why you chose to be alone.

The words filled his head despite his determination to keep them out. Tonight's incident had nothing to do with his attitude to relationships, but the thought came, anyway, and belatedly he tried to force himself away from the brink.

'No.' Chrissy's arms tightened around him. 'No, Nate. No stepping back this time. Please.'

'Dear God, Christianna. I should drive you home. If you stay—'

'I know.' Her gaze flared. A thousand slivers of knowledge coalesced in the liquid pools of her eyes. 'I know what will happen if I stay, Nate, and I'm not leaving.'

And then there was nothing but him and her, wrapped in flaring desire and agonising need.

'Take me to your bedroom, Nate.' She cupped his face in her hands. 'I know what I'm doing. I know what I want, and

what I want is you. Tonight. Everything I can have for thi
one night.'

He groaned. 'I want you, too. I want to strip you slowl
and see everything I reveal. I want to touch you, caress you
know you.' He shuddered. Wondered if this was madness. Bu
he couldn't let it go. Not any more.

'Then kiss me now.' Her words flared through him as the
moved into the bedroom, paused beside the bed. 'Kiss me lik
you really mean it. Like you couldn't possibly wait anothe
moment for it.'

He laughed low and harsh, a sound straight out of his need
'Don't you know that's how it is? I couldn't mean it more.
need you. Tonight…changed things. Changed me. I've los
the power to fight this, Chrissy.'

'I've lost that power, too.' Her mouth softened, her gaz
softened as well, receiving him in spirit even before he coul
make it reality. 'I need you, Nate. So much. Please don'
deny me any longer. Just this night….'

He moaned and lost the fight once and for all. He fell o
her mouth as though the very elixir of life could be foun
within. Maybe it could, because that first press of his lips t
hers sent a wave of heat from his toes all through his body.

'Nate. Yes.' Her responding shudder was accompanied by
low moan, and she pressed close, so close, the fabric of he
gown no barrier to the shape of her, the warmth of her agains
him.

He would remember that sound, that feeling of her pressin
close, forever. A shuddering breath filled his lungs and a wall o
emotion welled up inside him. And his heart said *yes. Yes, yes*

Her mouth made love to his, caressed and cajoled an
filled him with the need to be more. To give more. To fin
more in her than he had found in life before.

His arms locked around her, held fast. He eased them b

force of will, conscious of the scrapes on her shoulder and arm. 'I don't want to hurt you.'

'You won't. You aren't. I hurt a lot more in other ways right now. I hurt for your touch. For you. Surely you know that.' She stretched up, tightened her arms around his shoulders, arched her body into his. 'Kiss me again, Nate. Kiss me again, and again, and again.'

He searched her eyes, looked at the kiss-swollen lips and needed her so much. Way too much.

Although Nate didn't caution her again, Chrissy saw the warning in his eyes.

This will change things. Stop it, before it's too late.

But her heart filled with the knowledge that it was already way too late.

I want it to be you, Nate. You're the one I've waited for, even before I met you. I'll never love like this again, so I'm going to take this night. Take it and hold it close for the rest of my life.

Maybe it would change him. The thought whispered through her senses, suggestive, beguiling. Maybe he would realise he wanted something more than his roaming lifestyle.

Fool! But right now she didn't care. She just couldn't. The decision was made, and she wouldn't go back. Not for anything. Tonight she would have all of him, even if just for a moment.

'Make love to me, Nate. We've avoided it, stopped speaking of it, but all we've done is mark time.' As she spoke, she pressed her palms flat against his chest, slid them slowly down and around, caressing the taut line of muscle, the indent of each rib. 'This had to happen. Please, let it be now.'

He searched her face for what felt like aeons, his arms tight bands of resistance that held, but refused to embrace. That enclosed, but didn't encompass.

Then control snapped. The slender thread of it broke loose, and he swooped. 'You had your chance to say no.'

Kisses rained over her neck, the sensitive skin of her chest above the sleeveless dress.

'You don't dress warmly enough for the weather.' He growled the complaint even as his fingers trailed beneath spaghetti straps, caressed the indentations above her collarbone.

'My coat was fur-lined. Faux fur, that is.' Bella had made most of their clothes since the day their parents left them. Had dressed them to their strengths, to their personalities.

The ache that came with her memories lasted only moments, because Nate was kissing her again, and how could she be sad about the past with his kisses warming her? With the sound of his harsh, uneven breaths mingling with her own?

'Come here.' He tugged her into his arms, and closed them around her in sensual promise.

'Are you going to eat me, Mr Wolf?' The piece of whimsy slipped out, but he only growled deep and low.

His blue eyes flashed. 'Are you brave enough to find out?'

'Yes.' Her smile faded. Slipped away. 'Yes.' She reached for first one cuff, then the other. Released the buttons, then pushed his shirt from his shoulders. 'I want to touch you. Learn you. I want to know it all.'

Her fingers toyed with the light V of hair on his chest, enjoyed the crisp springiness.

He sucked in a sharp breath. Clenched his fists against her back, then his fingers splayed to begin their own journey of exploration. Along the ridges of her spine. Down over her buttocks and thighs.

Slumberous eyes linked with hers, but a fire burned in their depths. A fire that was just for her.

'Take your dress off.'

The silky demand came through clenched teeth, and for the first time she hesitated.

Behemoth Bum wasn't something she had thought about exposing. Until now. 'Turn the light out.'

'Not while there's breath in my body.' The fire was still there, but the touch of his finger beneath her chin was gentle. 'Never. Not when I can look at you, can see what I've thought about, imagined. Longed for.'

His mouth was tight. His gaze tracked over her before returning to meet hers. 'You're beautiful and I want to see every part of you. To touch all of you. Let me.'

That easily, he stripped her of her last defence. She nodded. Stood shaking in his arms as the dress slid to the floor.

His hands shaped each part of her, shoulders, arms, waist, back, so carefully, so tenderly, that she almost cried.

'What is it?' His mouth pressed to hers, suckled her lower lip and slowly released it. Worshipped that part of her as his hands explored reverently.

'It's nothing.' *It's everything. I hadn't realised how this would be. How much I would feel. How strongly it would move me. Even wanting you so much... I didn't realise.*

He kissed her again, a building desperation in every movement of his mouth. Her lips clung to his, followed his. A reflection of what she felt inside. Of how much she needed to meld with him. To be closer than any closeness she had known. Would it be that way for him? Different? More?

Doubts filtered in, made their presence felt. 'Will this be good? Will we both—?'

'We'll please each other, I promise.' He showed her how much they could do that. Praised every part of her as he explored her body with almost desperate thoroughness. Shuddered when she clung to him. Fanned her hair across his pillow and begged her not to let him hurt her as his body strained with leashed need.

That plea was more than concern for the newness of this.

For the fact that she had had no other lover. *I will never have another lover.*

The thought was fierce. Deep. Almost harsh in its intensity. He met that harsh fierceness with utter urgency.

And then she couldn't think at all, could only feel as Nate loved her with trembling hands and fierce single-mindedness. Broken endearments poured over her as he lost himself in their loving. She clutched those precious words close as tears rose in her eyes and spilled over.

Joy and pain mingled, and then there was only joy. Such joy as they found their completion together.

He bathed her afterward, soft, soothing strokes as her eyelids fluttered and a deep languor stole over her. Then he wrapped something soft and warm around her. One of his shirts, she realised as he eased her arms into it and took care of the buttons.

She wanted to speak. To share the feelings that even now swelled inside her heart. But her body fought her, dragged her farther and farther into the deep stillness of slumber. She was almost there when the light clicked off and Nate climbed into the bed beside her.

'Sleep, my darling.' His voice held a roughened edge, as though something harsh had scraped across his vocal cords. The clasp of his arms was strong, almost feverish before he drew a deep breath and seemed deliberately to relax his grip. 'I want this night in your arms. I can't bear...not to have it.'

'I'll give you...anything.' Mumbled words. She pressed her nose into his chest, inhaled the scent of him. Anything more taxing than breathing was out of her range right now. And then she slept.

I'll give you anything. Even in the deepness of his sleep, Chrissy's words tumbled through Nate's mind.

He drifted up through layers of consciousness. To full

awareness of his surroundings. Of darkness filtered through by moonlight. Of Chrissy tucked against his body, her curves soft and beautiful even beneath the ugliest shirt he owned.

How much time had passed? An hour? Forever? *I can cover you up*, he thought, *but it won't make me forget.*

Their lovemaking was etched in his mind, was threaded through his senses. Desperation and stark need had possessed him. Had taken him completely out of control, to some place where he could only feel. All his need for her. The sharp, aching knowledge that life would never be the same without her.

He raised a hand to stroke her hair. Just that, and his body trembled once again. Dear God, what had happened to him?

I can't let her go.

The starkness of the thought made him tense all over. Their lovemaking had been equally intense. She had looked into his eyes with nothing but trust, had given all of herself freely.

Even in that overwhelming intensity, he had loved her the same way. Fully and completely in a way that was foreign to his experience.

She murmured in her sleep and ran one soothing hand across his chest, as though she sensed his turmoil and wanted to calm it. Twined a long, shapely leg against his pyjama-clad one.

What had he thought? That clothing would actually be a barrier once sleep left him? That it would protect him? Or her? He wanted her again. Right now. And again and again and again. *I don't want to let her go.*

He could put down roots for her. He wanted to believe he could do that. Wanted it all, suddenly and fiercely, with such strength that a soft gasp escaped him. The whole marriage, family, share-a-home-together thing danced in his head, enticed him.

I have to let her go. Let her go, or stay with her and watch it all turn in on her, break down on her. Watch it hurt her.

'Nate? What's wrong?' A sleepy question, the words slurred as she struggled to wake properly.

'Nothing's wrong.' What a lie. It was all wrong, was all so out of control that it scared him. He had wanted her so desperately, so fiercely and with such primitive need, that he had taken her without remembering protection.

If she conceived… 'Go back to sleep.'

He stroked her arm, her hair, deliberately soothing her back to the comfort of sleep. Now wasn't the time for talking. If he was honest, he wasn't ready to face that. When she slept soundly again, clasped tight in his arms, he lay in the moon-limned night and faced how truly vulnerable this night had made him.

And slowly, as morning approached, he pulled his defences back together and reminded himself of all the reasons that walking away was the best thing he could do for her.

CHAPTER TWELVE

'You should leave, Nate. Go back to your overseas work straight away. Get your replacement in and I'll take care of Henry. It would probably be best for both of us if we didn't have to see each other again.'

Oh, brave words! But in truth, Chrissy spoke so that Nate wouldn't have to. So that she didn't have to hear him tell her that last night had been fun, but he was over it now, and hoped she was, too.

His determination to leave was etched in every taut line of his face, in the tightness of his shoulders beneath the soft grey shirt. She couldn't pretend it away.

And it wasn't as if she hadn't known. The moment she had woken this morning and realised he wasn't in the bed beside her, the whole thing was sealed. Later she would examine the hurt cascading through her.

'Let me get you some coffee.' His words were flat, careful, almost toneless. So different from the way he had spoken her name last night as he loved her.

Don't think of it. She sipped the coffee he handed to her. Glanced around the kitchen of Henry's cottage and wondered why she had thought she would survive this. Would be able to spend a night in his arms then walk away unscathed.

You thought it because your need for him obliterated everything else. You still need him. Need him and love him. That's why you hurt so much.

Nate had risen long before her. Had been dressed and waiting when she joined him in the kitchen after she showered. She felt foolish in last night's dress, and vulnerable because she had buttoned his shirt over it.

At the time, it had seemed a sensible idea. But that was before she entered the kitchen and memories of last night's ecstasy melded with the look of harsh rejection on his face to torture her.

'I'll get a taxi back to the apartment.' She set the coffee down and stood, unwilling and perhaps unable to prolong this. He mustn't think her needy. Or desperate. She didn't want him to think of her that way. Not ever. Pride told her to show her backbone and walk from this with her head high.

Yet her heart begged her to wade even further into these feelings. To embrace them utterly, no matter how much it might hurt. To hope, to believe that there could be a future for them.

She had entertained that thought last night. And had received the proof this morning that her imaginings had been just that. Fantasies. Groundlessly optimistic hopes that never had a chance of coming true.

If she gave in to those hopes again she would never get over them. They *would* swallow her whole.

'I'll drive you to the apartment.' For the first time, emotion showed. For just a tiny moment, he looked as devastated as she felt.

Then he blinked and she decided she had imagined that desperate look. Had conjured it up because it would have pleased her to see it. Would have given her hope. She didn't need hope right now. She needed strength. 'I'd prefer to take a taxi, but thank you for the offer.'

She forced her lips to relax. To turn up at the corners into some semblance of good cheer. 'Don't feel bad about last night, Nate. I wanted us to make love. You wanted it, too. We did, and I don't regret the experience. I hope you don't, either, but now it's over. We both know that.'

It was what he had to be thinking himself, so why wasn't he smiling? Letting out a relieved breath and saying thanks, and I'll call that taxi for you?

'Just like that?' His mouth was hard, flat, but his eyes burned. Seared her with some deep emotion. Some intense feeling that he clearly didn't intend to share. 'One night and that's the end of it? We put it behind us and forget about it?'

'I realise it's…awkward.' Heartbreaking, but she wasn't about to admit that to him. 'That's why it would be better if you left Australia right away.'

'I'm not going.' Just that, said in the harshest of tones. His brows drew down. The mouth that had kissed her with such stark intent tightened. Then, 'I won't leave until the problems at Montbank's are solved. You could still be in danger, and after last night you might be…' He didn't finish the thought.

'Pregnant? I won't be. It's too late in my cycle.' She refused to even consider a child that he wouldn't want to know. She laughed, a harsh burst of sound that died as quickly as it came.

Oh, she was in danger all right, but the danger was standing right before her. 'I won't be in any more danger than I would if you were still here.'

In fact, she would be in less, because she wouldn't have to struggle through the days in his company. It had been bad enough before last night. Now it was simply impossible.

'It's not just that.' His fists clenched at his sides. 'A lot has happened. I think we're close to learning just what's been going on in the company, and at the docks. Henry still needs to accept the idea of retirement. I can't leave until all that is resolved, and I need to be sure…' Again, he trailed to a stop.

'I see.' *You need to be sure that I don't carry your child.* She tried one last time. 'You could explain the situation to the new man. He could head up the investigations as you've been doing, work temporarily in the chair until Henry accepts the idea permanently—'

'That wouldn't be good enough.' He turned sharply. Walked the few paces to the sink and spread his hands against the bench on either side of it. 'Accept it. Accept it the way you've accepted that last night was all you wanted or needed.'

Yes, Nate. Last night was all I wanted. It's just that I still want it, and will go on wanting it while ever I have breath in me. I want a lifetime of last nights. Of being held in your arms and cherished, of feeling as though we've finally found some peace together. I need that, and I know I cannot have it.

'There is no more for us than last night.' She shrugged, a study in feigned nonchalance. 'You made your feelings clear.' An unsteady breath came and went. 'Or are you saying that you've changed? That you *want* to stay—?'

'I can't.' He swung around. Lifted his hands toward her, then stopped. Dropped them to his sides. 'God knows, I can't.'

He had brought this topic up. Had forced the conversation until she lost control and sought the one answer she wanted above all others. Be damned if she would let it go now, without fully understanding his reasoning.

'God may know, but I'm unfortunately not privy to the inner workings of your mind.' She waited, watching him, demanding with her silence and her gaze that he reveal the truth.

'You want your pound of flesh, don't you?'

Gritted words. Entirely the wrong images. She nodded. 'I'm going to have to work at your side after this, until *you* deem it time that you leave. I think that earns me the right to the truth.'

He didn't respond immediately. If the turbulence on his face was any indication, he probably wouldn't. But then he muttered, 'What the hell, anyway?' and left the kitchen to stride purposefully toward his grandfather's bedroom.

A moment later he returned with a photo frame clasped in his hand. He thrust it at her and stepped back as though simply touching it brought pain, or anger, or maybe both.

She dropped her gaze to the frame. Frowned at the unfamiliar face and, looking again, saw the likeness. 'Your mother.'

'My father left her—left us—when I was a baby.'

'I'm sorry.' Henry hadn't spoken of his daughter. Why hadn't she realised that until now? 'Do you hear from your father now, or see him?'

'No. I figure if he gave so little of a damn about us, what's the point?'

Chrissy understood those feelings. Understood his pain. 'What happened to your mother?'

'She committed suicide when I was eight years old. Put me in a taxi to Henry's house, then filled herself with pills.' A harsh, humourless laugh. 'I guess I wasn't enough to make it worth her sticking around, either.'

'Oh, Nate, no.' It couldn't have been that. 'I'm sure there must have been some other reason—'

'No reason other than that I curse every relationship I'm in.' His eyes bored into hers. 'I hurt the people I care about. They're better off when I stay away. That's why last night was a mistake, Chrissy. We were both feeling raw, and we let things get out of control, but it can't happen again.'

It can't happen again. That was the way Nate had summed up their night of lovemaking.

The memory was no more palatable ten days later. Chrissy acknowledged the thought as she forced herself to re-enter the

Montbank building. Ten days hadn't been anywhere near enough time for her to come to terms with that one night of passion, and all it had done in her heart, her spirit, her soul.

Every day she seemed to break a little more, yet the stubborn man would not leave until he got answers to the problems going on in the firm. How could she try to get over him if he wouldn't go away?

And what if some of her other feelings lately, some particular physical symptoms, for instance, were the result of more than stress?

'It *is* just stress. Get over it.' The lift lurched when it came to a stop, and her stomach lurched right along with it. Lunch, she acknowledged as she hurried toward her office, didn't appear to be agreeing with her.

Oh, God, please don't let me be pregnant.

Oh, God, please, yes. I want to be pregnant with his child.

Nate had tried to apologise and explain. To assure her that he had never overlooked such a thing before. A part of her had rejoiced that he had lost control enough for that to happen, but she had brushed his explanations off. Had assured him again that it was too late in her cycle for anything to happen.

Now she was late, late in her cycle. *It's just a few days. The typewriter went to the end of the page, and someone forgot to hit carriage return, that's all.*

At two p.m. Nate threw down his pen and stalked to face her desk. 'You don't look well. Do you need to go home?'

'I'm fine.' After that, she mopped her clammy forehead when he wasn't looking, took very small sips of water to ease the dryness in her mouth and watched the hands of the clock on the wall creep past each minute and hour in slow, miserly movement.

She didn't want to go home and crawl into her bed, with nothing to do but think of him and feel miserable. How would that help anything? Besides, she could manage this slight nauseous feeling. She was managing it just fine!

At a little before five, Nate went into the kitchenette and made tea. Brought her cup to her and placed it on the desk. 'Maybe this will help.'

Instantly, an eddy of revolted reaction began deep in her stomach and quickly rose.

'Thank you, I…' She pushed to her feet, swayed as the room swirled and her stomach contracted in desperate urgency. With her fist pressed to her mouth, she ran for their private bathrooms. Shoved through the door of the ladies' room.

When the retching finished she leaned, shaken, tears streaming down her face, against the washbasin. Nate's strong, tanned hand turned on the tap and rinsed the basin.

She cleansed her mouth and his hand appeared in front of her again, a wad of paper towels held in his fist. He gently mopped the tears from her eyes and dried her face. Their gazes met in the mirror, and slowly he turned her toward him.

'I can't believe you saw that.' She wanted to shrink into herself and stay there forever. She wanted to run to the nearest chemist's and buy a pregnancy-testing kit! Or maybe go home and crawl into bed, after all. Yes. Act as if it wasn't happening. That was a good choice right now.

'Do you think it's finished?' His question was as grim as the expression on his face.

She nodded. Grasped at straws. 'It could have been lunch. I've been feeling off ever since I got back from my break, and I feel just fine now. Maybe I just needed to get rid of something that didn't agree with me.'

His silence didn't exactly inspire further theorising. It didn't surprise her when they stepped back into her office and he immediately closed and locked the outer door, and punched the button to divert their calls.

Before she got anywhere near her desk, he took both their cups of tea and dumped them in the sink in the kitchenette. She heard the sound of running water.

When he came back, she had eased herself into her chair. Her legs weren't exactly steady, but she wished she didn't have the disadvantage of looking up at him.

Maybe he sensed that, because he sat on the corner of her desk before he took one of her chilled hands in his. 'Was that the first time?'

'Yes.' And it still didn't have to mean she was pregnant. If she had been feeling somewhat less than excited about anything other than bland porridge with a dash of lemon juice for the last couple of days, well, that could be some bizarre co-incidence, too.

Who eats porridge with lemon juice, let alone for every available meal?

She had given in and eaten a sandwich at lunch today because it just seemed too ridiculous to pack a Thermos full of porridge for work. This was what she got for it.

'You're cold right through.' He chafed her hand between his, examined her face, which no doubt looked hideously blotched.

Why did throwing up always make you cry? She hoped fervently that she wasn't about to get very familiar with the act.

'Are you pregnant, Chrissy?'

There it was. Out in the open. The simple question tore at her heart.

With each day that passed without her period turning up, she had avoided thinking about it. She had avoided her sisters, too, because she was scared they might somehow figure out all that had happened, and what she now feared. Yet it wasn't all fear.

I want his baby. I want it more than anything, and I've only just now realised it.

'I'm not sure if I'm pregnant or not.' Simply saying it made it seem more real. More possible, instead of just some faraway thought with no link to reality. 'I'm only a few days late.' She was usually very regular, so maybe she really was—

'What I want you to do is wait here.' He spoke slowly, carefully, as though even a raised voice would break her. 'Just rest in the chair. Don't try to do anything.'

'Where are you going?' She had thought he would want to talk about it, although she didn't want to think about what exactly he might say.

'I'm going to get an early-pregnancy test kit.' He shrugged. 'It's not exactly something I've bought before, but I'm sure I'll be able to work it out.'

And then he would expect her to use it. Just like that. Right now. Before she had adjusted to the possibility, had got her thoughts together. 'I...um—'

'Just wait.' He turned for the door, strode toward it then looked back. 'Quietly. I don't want to come back and find that you've fainted on the floor or something.'

His own words seemed to give him pause. In fact, his face paled in a way it hadn't even when he was in the bathroom with her, coping with her sickness. 'Maybe leaving isn't such a good idea.'

And then, in an act that she could only believe was borne out of a complete if momentary lapse into utter insanity, he reached for the phone on her desk and began punching in numbers. 'I'll get Gloria to run out for the kit.'

She got her finger over the disconnect button so fast that her head swam, but she made sure he didn't get through with that call. 'I really don't think it would be a good idea to ask our floating Jill-of-all-trades to step out for a pregnancy test for us.'

For a moment he simply blinked at her. Then he stared at the phone as if he had no idea how it had got into his hand.

Last of all he replaced it in its cradle with the sensitivity a bomb-squad expert would use when choosing that oh-so-vital 'right' wire to snip. 'I must have lost my mind.'

'That was my theory.' At another time, it would have been funny, but somehow, funny wasn't a reaction she related to this situation. 'Thank you for looking after me back there, Nate, but I can do the test myself. Buy the kit myself. Tomorrow will be soon enough—'

'If that's a joke, I'm not laughing.'

'Well, I'm not going to faint.' A hint of petulance crept into her tone. 'I might die of thirst and I'd really kill for a bottle of orange juice right now, but I'm not going to fade onto the carpet. Trust me.'

He looked her over, frowned at what he saw then pinched his mouth together and nodded. And then he strode out the door, almost knocking it off its hinges in his haste to get through it.

Nate completely rattled was something new to her. She pondered it as she busied herself with a dictation tape not yet finished. Sit and wait for him to come back? She wouldn't leave the building. That would be cowardly, but she saw no reason to count the seconds, either.

She would rather keep her mind occupied. Her attempts weren't entirely successful, but she had made good progress on the tape when a junior official from the stevedore company phoned.

Forget ignoring the phone until Nate got back, too. She almost wished she had left the phone alone, though, when the fool on the other end of the line kept insisting that she had sent him an email asking that he provide her with a copy of a cargo manifest.

'That's simply not true,' she told him for the third time. 'I would surely remember if I had done such a thing, and I haven't.'

The man ended the call with a terse grunt. Seconds later a copy email appeared in her inbox. It showed every sign of having originated from her! Five minutes of searching revealed nothing. On an off chance, she started a search through the computer's trash storage.

'Bingo. My God. Somebody did send that email, but it certainly wasn't me.'

'What are you doing working? I told you to rest.' Nate strode into the room, slapped the door shut and locked it again. 'At least you've got some colour in your face now.'

'There's something fishy going on with my email.' Keeping her gaze determinedly averted from the items in his hands, she started to tell him. 'It could even have to do with what's happening at the—'

'Later.' He cut her off. 'Frankly, I don't care if your computer just crashed and burned and you lost every file we've ever had. This is way more important.'

He handed her the paper chemist's bag. 'Here's the kit. You can have the juice when you come back with that test strip. Straight back, understand? We're going to watch for those little lines *together*.'

And that terse instruction pretty much wiped every other thought from her mind. Except one completely inane one. 'How do you know so much about the test?'

'I read the instructions on the way back.'

Oh, great. Visions of him wandering through the building studying that very obvious little box crashed through her head.

He took her elbow and tugged her from her chair. 'Discreetly. I read it discreetly.' Almost as an afterthought he went to the water dispenser in the corner of the room and pulled a plastic cup from it. 'You'll—ah—you might need this. The container in the kit seems kind of small for a—ah—for a lady to use.'

'Right.' So in she went to the bathroom again, only this time with a face that you could have fried a steak on. She avoided her gaze in the mirror as she opened the paper bag with trembling fingers. It took three reads of the instructions before she could get them to make sense. Her problem, not the manufacturer's.

Finally she knew what she had to do, and what to watch for, and she took care of business, disposed of the plastic cup, laid the strip over the mouth of the smaller container as suggested in the kit instructions and carried strip, container, empty kit and paper bag out into the office.

There. Done. Now all they had to do was wait. Possibly for five long, agonising minutes.

Nate was pacing the room. He stopped and turned toward her, a look of almost predatory interest on his face. 'You took long enough. I was about to come in there.'

'It took a while to read the instructions. I didn't want to mess it up.'

He reached her side quickly. Relieved her of the paper bag and remaining kit bits and pieces.

Peripherally she was aware that he set them down on her desk, but her gaze was locked on the strip resting over the cup. Her hand began to shake.

Instantly he clasped his over it, stabilising her, holding the cup and strip steady with her. He stood so close she could feel his breath stirring her hair, could feel his body warmth reaching out to her.

Oh, dear lord. What if she *was* pregnant? Well, she would just deal with it. A baby of Nate's would be a wonderful thing. Someone to love that was part of him.

'I can raise a baby.' She wasn't aware that she had muttered it aloud until Nate spoke.

'Let's get the test done first of all.'

Cautious. But what had she expected?

Stop panicking. There'll probably only be one line on the strip and the whole thing will have been a false alarm. Hit carriage return, scare over.

So why didn't she believe that? Why did she have a sudden deep and very strong conviction about what was going to turn up on that little strip?

Nate's hand tightened almost painfully on her wrist. A sharp inhalation of breath sounded above her bent head. 'Two lines. We've got two lines.'

Her vision wavered, and she blinked to bring it back into focus. On two strong, sturdy lines that were darkening by the second. *Pregnant. I'm pregnant.* 'Looks like the little sucker has given me a strong hCG level already.'

Darn, had she really said that? In her horrified silence, Nate's bark of laughter reverberated around the room.

Again, colour stole into her face. Yes, she *had* said that. Swift remorse filled her. All the blood seemed to rush just as quickly from her face to her toes, and tears filled her eyes.

She was having a baby and the first thing she'd done was call it a name and blame it for upsetting her hormone levels. 'I wasn't ready. The words just came out.' As these ones did, choked and husky.

Nate's laughter faded, the test stick and cup were taken from her and then his hands held her arms.

Would their baby have Nate's long-fingered hands? Would Nate ever want to see the child they had created? 'I'm sor—'

'Don't.' He laid a finger over her lips. 'This possibility has been in my mind since the night at the cottage. If you want to blame someone, then I'm the one for it because I should have protected you. Truthfully, I'd rather focus on what happens next.'

Awe filled his voice and he swallowed hard. 'We're having a baby.'

She couldn't absorb his jubilation. Could only focus on the fact that she was indeed going to have a baby, but Nate didn't want to be around, let alone become a father, and how would she tell Henry about this? And her sisters?

Yet a corner of her heart hugged the knowledge tightly. Nate's baby. A child made from that one night when, for just a little while, all barriers had been down.

That surge of love swelled and she finally looked at him with a clear gaze. 'I know you don't want family life, but I guess I do, because I want this baby. I'll care for it. If you want to see it sometimes, we'll arrange it somehow—'

'Is that how you think this will go?'

If she didn't know him so well, she would believe it was pain she saw in his gaze. 'I guess, that is, I suppose I assumed... What do you think will happen, then?'

CHAPTER THIRTEEN

'WE GET married. Raise the child together. It's the only responsible thing to do.'

Nate spoke almost harshly, but inside him a well of something that felt startlingly like jubilation had begun. That shout of laughter earlier hadn't been simple amusement at Chrissy's sarcastic comment.

He was going to be a father. He and Chrissy had made a child. They would *have* to stay together now. He wouldn't have to lose her. He would care for her and the baby, always. 'This child deserves two parents, don't you think? Since two of us created him or her?'

The future kaleidoscoped through his mind, image after image. Watching Chrissy grow large with their child. Being with her for the birth. Making that home together that he had forbidden himself. 'There's no choice now. It's too late to try to do things differently.'

Henry would be a great-grandfather. Nate's grin widened. The old man would love that. If anything could give him the lift he needed, then surely a great-grandchild would do it.

And what about you, Nate? You promised yourself you wouldn't hurt Chrissy, and now you're trying to tie her to yourself for life.

His jubilation faded. OK, so maybe their future wouldn't remain rosy forever, but he wanted a chance. Maybe he could find some way...

'There are a thousand choices aside from a forced marriage with no love involved and that's only been offered because a baby happened into the picture!'

Chrissy crammed the test stick and cup into the paper bag, then hauled out her shoulder bag and shoved the lot inside. 'Yes, there are plenty of choices, Nate Barrett, and I choose *not* to marry you. I refuse to be trapped in a marriage that you felt forced to offer!'

'But you can't...' Belatedly, he realised that his announcement that they should marry could have been put in more digestible terms. Could have been a little more encouraging, and a little less as though he had accepted his life sentence.

'As far as I'm concerned, Nate, we *have* talked. You've tossed out your little decree, and I've turned it down.' She skirted the desk and him, giving him the widest berth possible, and headed for the locked outer door of the office.

He followed her to the door. Reached for her hand. 'Chrissy, wait. You've misunderstood.'

'I can't.' The glitter of tears in her eyes cut all the way through him. Sliced his heart into pieces because she looked so hurt, so unhappy. 'I need—I need to go home. I need to talk to my sisters. I need to be with people I love and who love me. Please...just let me go.'

I need to be with people I love and who love me.

After she had left, he stayed numb for who knew how long, those words reverberating in his head. Was there no chance for him, then? Did she not love him even the tiniest little bit?

What is it you really want, Barrett? If you want to be a husband and a father and do it right, that means staying. Forever. You always said you wouldn't do that.

But this was Chrissy, and the child they had made together. This was different.

Nate sat at his desk. He even did some work, but his heart wasn't in it. Because, he realised, his heart was with her. The knowledge filled him. He loved Chrissy Gable. Loved her in a way he had never expected to love anyone.

Loved her and had used her pregnancy as an excuse to demand that she stay with him. To force her into commitment even though he had no idea how to make a relationship between them work.

He had fallen in love with the mother of his child.

The pencil in his hand snapped in two. He stared at it without a shred of comprehension. He needed to go after her. To talk to her. Tell her how he felt and ask her to help him not to hurt her. There had to be a way.

On his desk, the phone shrilled. He glanced at the clock. Realised very little time had passed, even though it seemed he had been sitting there forever. He almost ignored the call, but at the last minute snatched it up. It could be a problem with Henry. 'Barrett.'

'Nate, it's Bella.' A sharp intake of breath. Then words tumbling over each other in almost hysterical haste.

'Chrissy's been in a car accident.' Bella named a busy junction a few minutes from the office.

Her voice cracked as she went on. 'There's a pile-up and I could hear sirens over the phone when she called me. I'm on the other side of the city and I'm going to have to get public transport. Soph's out of town again. Chrissy says she's fine. She was babbling about pot-plant shopping—I don't know why. But she's trapped in the car, Nate. Maybe she feels fine because she's lost her legs, or she's about to die of blood loss, or—'

'Bella!' His sharp tone stopped the outpouring of fear. It didn't stop him from imagining each of the things she had named, and more. 'Dear God.' His body clenched and all the blood rushed from his head.

For a second he thought he was actually going to pass out. He forced breath into his lungs. 'I'll go to her. I'll get through somehow.'

He was running for the car park before he realised he had banged the phone down in Bella's ear without waiting for a response. She would just have to understand. The woman he loved, the mother of his unborn baby, needed him.

'Chrissy. Dear God.' He ran faster.

Nate probably broke every traffic law in the state during the drive from the company building to the scene of the accident.

Traffic was being directed around the problem area, and police and a single ambulance vehicle were on the scene.

With no thought for anything but Chrissy, he drew the convertible as much to the side as he could manage and jumped out.

'Hey, man, are you crazy?' someone shouted after him. 'You can't leave your car in the middle of the street like that.'

'Park it for me.' He tossed the keys over his shoulder. 'I'll get it later.'

Putting it from his mind, he forced his way between the cars until he reached a crumpled yellow bug with a P-plate sitting forlornly in its rear window. His eyes filled with tears and he rushed to the car, arms spreading on the roof as he peered inside, terrified of what he might find.

'Off the road, please, sir. This isn't a spectator event.' A police officer gave him the white-glove treatment. Arm stretched, he indicated the pavement with stoic command.

Nate frowned at the officer. Stared again at the car and finally comprehended that Chrissy wasn't in it. 'Where have they taken the—the injured? Have most of the ambulances already left?'

The officer gave him an odd look, then pointed again to the pavement to the left. Nate gave up and strode toward the ambulance.

All the other ambulances must have left with their patients already. He would ask, quickly, find out where Chrissy had been taken, and go to her.

His gaze searched the street briefly and he spotted his car parked way down on the left. He nodded, relieved that his urgency hadn't robbed him of transport.

'I shouldn't have let her drive with so little experience.' What if she wasn't OK? He could lose her and their baby. How would he survive that? He wasn't sure he could. 'She's never driving again. When I find her, I'm going to tell her—'

'Nate. What are you doing here?'

Chrissy's voice. Clear. Familiar. *Near.*

He turned his head. Found her a few feet away from the ambulance. She had been giving details to a police officer, and now tucked her wallet back inside her shoulder bag and walked toward him. On her own legs, which appeared to be in working order.

'You're… Are you all right? The baby? Your car's a write-off. It's a wonder you didn't die. Bella said you were trapped.' He stopped, cursed himself for voicing the fears. Stared as tears formed in her eyes and fell. There. See? He'd upset her.

'Oh, God, Chrissy, I'm sorry.' He wrapped his arms around her, hugged her to him. 'Only, why aren't you in one of the ambulances and on your way to a hospital by now? Why have they left you to fend for yourself like this?'

She leaned into the hug for a moment, then drew back a little to look up at him. 'I'm not hurt, Nate. It was just a knock-on. Didn't you see? We made a fair sort of commotion between all of us, but nobody was hurt beyond maybe a bit of shock or something.'

Again, he struggled to understand. He turned, not easing his grip, and stared once more at the mess on the road. Cars had been, and were, in the process of being towed away.

Now that he looked at the bug again, he could see that it had weathered the excitement with little more than a smashed windscreen and a bit of minor front and rear damage. With Chrissy held in his arms, he could comprehend that the damage hadn't been as bad as he had at first believed.

'A problem at the front of the line of traffic, and you were one of the cars behind that had nowhere to go.' A simple intersection smash-up. 'The cars were probably moving at a crawl at the time.'

'Yes, thankfully.' She nodded, and he forced his arms to ease their grip on her, although he didn't let go completely.

A touch of pride entered her tone. 'I didn't wrench the wheel or panic. I just tried to control Gertie as best I could, like Joe said to do if I ever got whacked from behind in traffic like this. The police officer said I kept my head and did what any really experienced driver would have done.'

'Right. That's good. You did good.' She had survived. That was the best achievement in his book. He searched her face. Restrained himself just barely from frisking her from head to foot to make sure for himself that she really wasn't damaged.

'You're really OK?' His voice roughened with the knowledge of how precious she was to him. 'You and the baby?'

'Chrissy. Oh, thank God.' Bella materialised beside them. Breathless and dishevelled, she snatched Chrissy into her arms and all but strangled her. Tears poured down her face as she did what Nate had wanted to—patted her sister down, checking with shaking hands to make sure everything was OK.

After a moment, Chrissy's hands wrapped around Bella's arms and tightened. 'Bella. Stop. I'm all right.' When that had no effect, Nate's beloved gave her sister a good shake. 'Bella! If your hands go any further south, I swear I'll…'

Bella stopped. Took a deep breath, and seemed to become aware of her surroundings again. Gave Chrissy one last pat for good measure, then drew back. Drew herself together in a display of strength that revealed just how tough these sisters were. Her love for Chrissy was somehow only underlined by that action.

Nate would have given anything for a family like the one formed by Chrissy and her sisters. Had thought he had found it, for a time, with his grandfather. Until Margaret had come along and it all went belly-up.

Chrissy turned to her sister. Bit her lip. 'I'm afraid Gertie took a bit of a beating. They wanted to tow her, but I reckon she'll still be drivable, and if there's work to be done Joe should be the one to do it. I called him. He should be here soon. My new plants are OK, although I worry about trauma to them.'

Bella cast her a confused look, but Nate understood. She had gone shopping for therapy after the shock of realising she was pregnant. Naturally, it would be plants that she bought.

Joe arrived. Soph phoned, returning an earlier distraught call from Bella, and insisted on speaking with both sisters, twice over, before she would even begin to accept that everything might be all right.

After a swift examination of the car while Nate glared repressively at him from the pavement, Joe drove off in it. Nate glanced toward his own vehicle.

'Here you go, mate. She's over there, safe and sound.' A bear of a man separated himself from a group who, from their leather gear and the well-known symbol on their jackets, appeared to be gang bikers.

He dropped a set of keys into Nate's hand. Gave what probably passed for a smile through a face full of beard. 'Motorbikes are me own choice. Hogs rock. But it didn't kill me to drive her off the road for ya, even if you did try to bean me with the keys.'

'Thanks.' Nate's eyes narrowed. 'Uh, I was a little preoccupied before. What's your name?' He reached for his wallet. 'Can I—?'

'Not unless you want me to break your bloody arms off so those ambos have something to do with themselves for real.' The man slapped him on the back hard enough to jolt him forward, then glanced at the two sisters standing staring at them. 'Couldn't fool me that she's breedin', though. Skinny as pretzels, both of 'em.'

With those profound words, he walked off.

Leaving Nate to face Chrissy and her sister. He bit down on the urge to share a few choice words that would match up to anything a biker could come up with.

Chrissy seemed too stunned to speak. Not so Bella. Her eyes widened, then narrowed, and she divided her gaze between her sister and him until it settled on him in earnest.

When she spoke, it was with the voice of the thousand waters sometimes used to describe God himself. *'You got my sister pregnant?'*

A screech from the cellphone in Bella's hand made him aware that Soph was still tuned in to the conversation as well.

'Ah, listen, Bella, this probably isn't the time or the place—'

'Be quiet.' Bella put the phone to her ear. Spoke clearly and concisely into it. 'You'll have to excuse me now, Sophia. Christianna and I have a *situation* to deal with. I'll call you later.'

* * *

It took almost an hour to extricate them from Bella's protective, outraged clutches. Chrissy's sister alternated between ranting at Nate, telling Chrissy she would be the best mother a baby had ever known, that she would be the best aunt in the world and crying.

Yes, Bella. Crying. All over the place. Strangely, Bella's reaction was just what Chrissy needed to pull herself together. In the end, she guided her sister to Nate's car, they all piled in and Nate drove them to the apartment.

He had taken Bella's hammering. Had accepted every bit of vitriol and had simply repeated, at relevant intervals, that he intended to make a future with Chrissy and they just needed time to work things out. Chrissy's heart leapt every time she thought about it. She tried not to hope too much, but...

When they stopped in the street outside the apartment, Chrissy got out with Bella, but motioned Nate to stay in the car. 'I need you to do something for me, Bella.'

'Anything.' Bella squared her shoulders and looked as though she would gladly shred every male in the population into tiny little pieces, if it was what Chrissy wanted.

Chrissy suppressed a smile. 'Will you please go and see Joe? Ask him what he thinks about fixing Gertie back up? And will you get my plants out of the car and give them some water and tell them they'll be OK now?'

'Why can't we both—?'

'Nate and I need to talk.' And she wanted her sister to be busy while that happened, so she would stop worrying, would calm down a little and regain some of the usual Bella perspective on life. 'I'm going to ask him to take me back to the office. I walked out in such a hurry this afternoon that I left things untidy, and it will give us a chance to settle a few things. Please give me that time, Bella. I need it.'

'OK.' Bella nodded. 'But you call me if you need me. I'll have my cell with me and I'll get to you—'

'I know. I love you.' They exchanged kisses, and Chrissy got back into the car.

Nate was waiting with his hands clenched on the wheel.

'You heard that?' She waited for his nod, then went on. 'I'd like to go back to the office. I left stuff strewn on my desk, and I guess you're right. We do need to talk.'

'We could go to the cottage. You should be in bed, or at the least on a sofa with your legs elevated or something.'

The strain hadn't left his voice, but who could blame him? Bella on a rampage had surprised even her, and she had grown up with her. 'I won't break, Nate, and the baby is as secure in there as it was when we did that test earlier.'

'OK. You're right. Sorry. I can't seem to think straight at the moment.' But he had no trouble handling the traffic, and soon had them heading for the office.

Something occurred to her, and she voiced it unconsciously. 'That biker guy. He said Bella and I were both skinny. How could he say that when I've got the Battle of the Barges Bum?'

'Your bottom,' Nate said through clenched teeth, 'is not a barge. It's…luscious. Erotic. Every man's fantasy. Did I act as though I didn't like it when we were in bed together making this child?'

The affront in his tone made her realise he was deadly serious. And a wave of surprise and, yes, pleasure rolled over her. The tenderness that came as she realised they truly had created this baby in those wonderful moments tightened her throat.

She cleared it carefully before speaking. 'You really like my bottom?'

'Since the day I first saw it. *You*, I mean. Since the day I *saw you*, and noticed it.'

'Oh. Well, I guess that's all right, then.' She settled back in her seat, but her mind raced. Today she had found out she was pregnant, and survived a car crash. Nate had found her and appeared to almost have lost his mind with fear for her.

And her sister had gone on a rampage the likes of which Chrissy had never seen before. She had survived all this— had powered through all this, really—and she felt amazing. Ten feet tall.

Strong enough, certainly, to solve a corporate mystery. Or to at least unravel another part of the puzzle. 'When we get to the office, there's something I want to show you.'

Nate muttered something about having a few things he would like to show *her*, like appropriate bottom appreciation, but she ignored him and hurried on.

'When you were out getting the pregnancy test, someone from the stevedore company phoned.' It was quite exciting, actually, now that she had the time to get excited about it. 'There's got to be a link between what he said and what's going on at the docks. If we search the tracking offices, cross-match the manifest he sent me, we might even discover who's behind this!'

Nate's excitement lacked spark, but he did condescend to listen to her properly as they travelled up in the car park lift and entered their now deserted floor.

'We'll investigate it.' He made the assurance as he strode ahead of her toward their offices. 'But we can do that after we talk. First, we have to settle our future. That accident today—'

He came to an abrupt halt just inside the door to their office suite. 'Margaret. What are you doing here?'

The words were rapped out as Margaret surged to her feet from her position at Chrissy's desk.

Chrissy gasped. 'She's using my computer. But why?' The

truth dawned on her, and fell from her lips as she stared into Margaret's glittering eyes. 'It was you. You're the one who's been interfering with our shipping.'

'Get back, Chrissy. Get behind me. She's— I don't think Margaret is feeling herself right now.' Nate's rough warning came as she realised the rest of it.

It was Margaret who had sent a thug to threaten Nate's life. Chrissy gasped, and outrage filled her. How dared this woman threaten harm to the man Chrissy loved? 'How could you, Margaret? You have a lot to answer for—'

'And you're in the wrong place at the wrong time.' Margaret whipped a diamond-studded purse into view and pulled a small pistol from it. 'This is all Henry's fault. If he hadn't put me on that ridiculous budget, saying I should love him more than his money—'

Her voice cracked. The gun wavered, and then she steadied her aim. Right at Chrissy. 'Actually, you're the cause of the trouble, really. Everything was fine before you came along and became so pally with my husband. He treated you like a saint. Talked about you all the time. He loved you more than he loved me.'

'That's not true, Margaret.' Nate eased himself forward, put his body between Chrissy and the barrel of the gun.

'Nate, no.' Chrissy gritted the warning, but he ignored it. She clutched the back of his suit jacket in trembling fingers. 'It's me she has the problem with. Let me face her. Try to talk to her.'

From what she could see of Margaret beyond Nate's broad shoulder, the woman was teetering on a shuddering edge. They had to help her—somehow.

Margaret proved how close to that edge she was a moment later when she began to cry—big, fat tears that rolled down her face and ruined her make-up.

'I can't live like a pauper. Don't you see? I'm made for

better things than that.' She raised her other hand in a pleading gesture. 'I was made for *you*, Nate. Not for some old man and his riches. Why didn't I realise I could have had you and your riches before it was too late?'

Chrissy gasped. Said in low tones, 'She's mad.'

'Give me the gun, Margaret, and we'll talk about this.' Nate took another step toward Margaret.

For a moment Chrissy stood frozen, convinced that Margaret would simply pull the trigger and kill Nate. Her heart stuttered at the thought.

Nate will talk her around. If anyone can do it, he can.

'Give me the gun, Margaret. Please, my dear.' Nate held out his hand, palm up. 'We can talk about anything you like, once you do that.'

Margaret held on to the gun, and gave a sage nod that made no sense. Her eyes were filled with a dark desperation that sent shivers down Chrissy's spine. 'You should have stayed away from the docks, Nate. I didn't want them to hurt you, but I had to get my little additions to Montbank's cargo safely away on those ships.'

'You must have been very clever to hide things on the ships, Margaret.' Nate made it sound like a compliment, and all the while edged toward the trembling woman. 'What did you hide? Was it drugs? Some other contraband?'

'Stolen jewellery and artefacts. Very small, very valuable pieces that could be hidden easily.' Her smile stretched across her teeth. 'I took them myself. From parties I attended. Nobody ever knew, and I've been happily supplementing my allowance. I *am* very clever, aren't I?'

Her mood shifted in an instant. Became brittle. 'It was the only answer, don't you see? But then, when you came back, I wanted you. I was certain this time I could convince you, but you wanted *her* instead.'

She spat the words, and the gun swung toward the door. Chrissy didn't have time to think. Nate simply threw himself across the table and knocked Margaret to the floor. He wrestled for control of the gun. A shot went off and Chrissy's whole world stilled.

'Nate!' She leaped forward, lifted the heavy phone set from her desk and raised it, ready to strike.

They were on the floor, Nate and Margaret. For a moment she didn't know which one was harmed, and then she realised neither had taken the bullet. It had blown a hole through the wall near her potted plants.

Margaret was no match for Nate's strength. He subdued her almost instantly, then eased to his feet, keeping Margaret's arms locked behind her in a tight hold.

The fight seemed to have gone out of Henry's wife. She stood with her head bowed, soft sobs wrenching her body. The woman appeared to have aged ten years in these few short moments, and a well of pity rose up in Chrissy. 'What will happen to her? How will we break this to Henry?'

'You'll co-operate with the police, won't you, Margaret?' Nate's voice was gentle. 'We'll get you the best care. People who will be kind to you and help you to see what a good person you are.'

Chrissy had never admired him more than she did in that moment, as he showed compassion to the woman who had forced him from the country six years ago, used his grandfather's company to aid her illegal dealings and had just aimed a gun at them both.

She swallowed hard and stepped forward. Spoke softly. 'I'll bet you had no intention of shooting either of us and you're already sorry that you pointed the gun our way, aren't you?'

Margaret nodded, sobbing. 'I didn't *want* to harm anyone.

I don't know why I did such wicked things. It all got out of my control.'

'You need help. We're going to get it for you, but you have to co-operate with the people who want to help you.' Nate motioned for Chrissy to get the gun.

She picked it up gingerly and, after a moment's study, put the safety lock on. 'I don't think it can discharge now.'

'Good. Call the police, will you, my love?' He gave Margaret a look of calm compassion. 'I kind of have my hands full.'

CHAPTER FOURTEEN

'WE'LL help you, Henry. You don't have to face any of this alone.' Nate's voice broke as he reached for his grandfather's hand. Covered it with his own. 'I'm so sorry that Margaret said those things at the police station. You have to understand she just… Her mind isn't quite right. She—'

'I already knew, Nate. I'm afraid I'm the one who needs to say sorry.' Henry's smile was sad, but he squared his elderly shoulders against the leather chair in his sitting room. 'I knew that my wife had chased after you, and that you left to try to save my pride. I pretended to know nothing about it because I didn't want to admit I'd made a terrible mistake.'

His sigh filled the silent room, and Chrissy closed her eyes, hurting for both of them.

'I let her chase you away from me.' Henry's eyes filled with tears. 'I've had my head in the sand, pretending nothing was wrong ever since.

'Please forgive me, lad. I should have let her go right after I married her. Now she needs help, and I'll provide for her, now and in the future, but I'm going to divorce her. She'll be happier on her own, and I don't want her coming between us any more.'

Nate pulled his grandfather into a fierce hug. When they

separated they both had tears in their eyes. Chrissy choked back the emotion in her own throat and got to her feet. 'I should leave you. You should have your privacy for this.'

'Stay.'

'Don't go.'

They spoke together. Grandfather and grandson, and turned twin determined gazes on her.

Nate got to his feet and came to her chair, raised her from it. 'I'm sure Henry would agree that he—that *we*, the Montbank family, need you.'

Henry nodded, but a twisted pain filled his face. 'There's more I have to say. I guess this is a night for confessions, but I...can't hold this back any longer. It's best you're both here when I say it.'

Nate's arms tightened around Chrissy.

She, too, tensed. 'Whatever it is, Henry, I'm sure it won't matter to us.'

'You're a generous girl. I've always liked that about you.' Henry sighed and shook his head. His words slowed a little, slurred the tiniest bit, revealing his strain. 'Things with Margaret, well, they were never what I had hoped for. Our relationship progressively worsened as time passed. I'm afraid while she was busy spending my money, I turned my unhappiness into a rather unhealthy addiction to the stock market.'

His voice dipped to a low mutter. 'At first it was just a dabble. But it didn't go well. I lost money, and I've never been good at accepting defeat. I kept thinking I could beat it if I could just get a break. Such obvious gambling justification, yet I let myself believe it.

'I put Margaret on a budget, but I should have realised it wouldn't work.' A deep sigh. 'It didn't stop *my* behaviour.'

Nate dropped one arm from around Chrissy, but tucked her

in against his shoulder. Gave his grandfather a gentle smile as realisation dawned on his face.

'You're the one who's been cooking the books. You did a pretty good job of hiding it, Gramps. I've had investigators on it for weeks, and they still haven't got it all worked out. Have we lost much?'

'You mean, has your grandfather lost much?' Henry shook his head. 'Enough, lad. Enough to make me realise I've been a fool and that it has to stop. I want you to buy me out. As you did with the overseas interest. You don't have to stay here, but I don't want to go back to management, either. It's no longer healthy for me to be there. I've finally accepted that.'

'And you're all right with it, aren't you.' It was a statement, and Henry nodded agreement.

'In the end, it'll be a relief to be able to stop worrying about it all.' He got slowly to his feet. 'Forgive a silly old man?'

'Already done.' Nate wrapped his arms around Henry again. Hugged him gently and pulled back. 'Forgive *me* for being stupid and wasting six years that I could have been closer to you? And promise me you'll get better?'

'Now that I've confessed my guilty secret, I expect my recovery will move along faster.' Henry's laugh was close to its previous hearty boom of sound. 'And there's nothing to forgive. You did what you believed was best.'

He moved toward the door. 'The files are in my office. You can take them any time you're ready. You'll see what I've done, what it all adds up to. Now, I think, if I've read matters correctly, that you two might also be in need of a little privacy.'

When they protested, he waved a hand. 'My night nurse has shown a surprising propensity for cryptic crossword puzzles. I think I might like to discuss her latest find with her. That is, if she's been game enough to bring it along tonight.'

As though his words had summoned her, a grey-haired woman poked her head around the door. 'Oh, I've been game enough all right, you old goat. Now, if you're finished blabbering in here, it's time for your dinner.'

'And the crossword?'

She took her time answering him, then gave in and nodded, a twinkle in her faded periwinkle eyes. 'All I'll say is that you'll need to know the difference between erotica and rotting trout if you want to get anywhere with this little gem.'

'An erotic cryptic puzzle, eh?' Henry snorted and headed for the door, a determined gleam in *his* faded eyes. 'I've been around longer than you have, Sally Smith, and I've studied my share of erotic art. I'm well-versed in the ancient texts, too. I'll give you a run for your money, don't you worry.'

He paused to draw a breath. 'Why haven't *you* retired yet, anyway? You've got to be past retirement age.'

'Compliments, compliments.' She tucked his arm into hers, and with that they began the slow ascent to Henry's first-floor bedroom. 'Maybe I haven't found anyone I'd like to spend my retirement with. I miss my Bert. It would take a special kind of man to replace him.'

Henry's eyes narrowed in contemplation. 'Or maybe just to understand that he's gone, and be a friend, eh?'

Nate frowned after them. 'I think my grandfather just stated his intentions to pursue his nurse.'

Chrissy raised a brow, a grin forming on her face. 'I think you may be right about that.' Her smile faded and she sighed. 'I hope he's going to be all right. At least Margaret is co-operating with the police. She was quite willing to tell them everything she knew, contact names, details of the items she stole and from whom…'

'Margaret is trying to do the right thing now, in her own

way. She'll always be selfish and vain, but maybe she'll find a way to be happier with herself.'

Nate paused. 'It hurt you to learn of Henry's gambling, didn't it?' He closed the sitting-room door and drew her down onto the couch. 'I'm sorry your idol turned out to have feet of clay, Chrissy. I know that must have been hard to hear.'

'It was.' In that first moment that Henry had admitted the truth, she had felt sick inside. Betrayed. Because she had looked up to him and thought of him as almost a surrogate father, and hadn't wanted him to let her down. 'I guess all people have failings.'

And who was she to judge Henry for his? 'He's still a good man, Nate. One of the best. He reacted that way because he needed Margaret to love him and *she* failed *him*.'

'Like your parents failed you?' He took her hands in his, stroked his thumbs across her knuckles. 'Tell me what happened, Chrissy, and why there's guilt in your eyes sometimes when you look at your sisters. And why it is that sometimes when they reveal they love you, you almost seem as though you think you don't deserve it? I know you love them in return, so…what is it?'

Only someone who cared deeply could have seen so much about her. In truth, she had worked very hard to hide the whole truth even from herself. Chrissy bit her lip.

'Trust me with it, Chrissy. Please.' His hands tightened on hers, and his eyes gazed deep into hers with such honesty, such promise, that she almost cried out.

'Because, you see—' he hesitated, took a deep breath and then plunged on '—I've realised that I'm in love with you, and, no matter what else we have to deal with to get there, I want to marry you and keep you in my life. I want to get rid of the barriers, Chrissy, so we can be together.

'I've been afraid, too, you see. That I would ruin our relationship if I stayed.' His chest expanded on a deep breath. 'But tonight has showed me it's not about that. Leaving Henry didn't help. It only made it worse, because he loved me and needed me, and I needed him.

'I realise now that I can care for him and it will only do him good, no matter what else is happening in his life at the time. I want to care for you the same way. I'm hoping that you might love me, too.'

'You want to care for me because of the baby.' Because of the child they had made, Chrissy told herself. Not because he loved *her*. Wanted *her*. He felt affection, not love. Not the real kind. The forever kind.

'You could have lost the baby in that car accident today.' His mouth tightened in pained remembrance. 'When I first got there, I don't know what happened to me, Chrissy, but Gertie… I thought you couldn't possibly have survived. She looked like a write-off. I guess because of my fear.'

He released her hands. Laid his gently over the flat tummy that even now cherished their child. 'I didn't want to have lost our baby, but I feared it. Most of all, I didn't want to have lost *you*. Marry me, Christianna Gable, and I *will* make you happy.'

His throat worked. 'We *can* be happy together, Chrissy, if we love each other. I've realised that now.'

It was a plea from his heart. She recognised that immediately, and if Nate was brave enough to put his past behind him and reach out for happiness with her, then she had to at least try to help him understand all that drove her. All that formed her feelings and thoughts about life and relationships.

She *wanted* a future with Nate. More than anything. But would she be enough to hold him and keep him happy? The only way to find out was to expose all her failings. If he still wanted her after that…

'I don't know if my problem is resolvable, Nate, but I want you to hear it, because I love you, too.' The liberation of simply putting it into words brought tears to her eyes. 'I love you and I do want a life with you. I'm just still not sure it's possible.'

'I'll help you to believe it.' He brought his mouth to hers. Kissed the taste of tears from her lips, wrapped his arms around her and stilled, his face buried in her hair. 'Talk to me. Let me into this last stronghold, and maybe we can break it down together.'

'All right.' She took a fortifying breath, drew back a little so she could look into his eyes as she talked.

'First of all, Bella and Soph believe that our parents left all of us because they just got sick of parenting.' She shuddered, and forced herself to continue the confession. 'But I was the one who ultimately drove them away. The one who was not bright enough, not talented enough, not interesting enough.'

She feigned an unaffected shrug. 'In comparison, Bella and Soph were always beautiful and artistic and remarkable. Our parents left all of us because they couldn't stand *me*. Had to get away from *me*, and I've never had the courage to tell my sisters the truth.'

A breath shuddered out, then another. 'I was afraid that Bella and Soph would be angry and leave me, too. Sometimes, when I look at them, I think about what they've lost because of me, and I feel guilty because they've lost it, and yes, I guess I feel less talented, less appealing, but I've tried to accept that. I love my sisters, and the rest is just…the way it is.'

'They're not better than you. Not more beautiful or talented or special or anything else!' The deep anger in his eyes demanded her attention. 'Have you looked at yourself? Really looked?' He flung a frustrated hand out. 'Have you looked inside your heart? Why do you think your sisters love you so much? It's because there's so much to love!'

Before she could attempt to respond, he went on.

'Your parents were stupid and selfish to leave.' His fists clenched. 'I don't know why they did it, but that was *their* fault, Chrissy. Not yours. And if they left because they thought you weren't as good or as special as the others, then they were twice the fools I already think them.'

His arms locked around her, as though he could hug away the years of hurt and confusion and blame if he simply held on long enough.

She fought back tears and forced herself to examine her thoughts, the feelings she had hidden away in places that might never have seen light if not for him. 'I'm not sure I know how you knew and understood all that, but I won't deny it. I guess I'm going to have to reassess my self-image a bit.'

The remainder of his anger drained away, and his arms relaxed a little. 'We've both been foolish, blaming ourselves for things that were out of our control.'

'Like your mother, and the problem with Margaret and Henry.' She nodded. 'Bella still had to take on a lot of responsibility, though, and Soph was so young.'

'And you all stuck together and came out of it stronger and better. Like I should have stuck with Henry.' His mouth lifted at one corner. A tiny whisper of tender encouragement. 'But in truth, don't you think if they only wanted to leave *you*, your parents would have simply shoved you into a boarding-school, taken the others and run? Have you ever considered that?'

At first, the idea was simply incomprehensible. Then she realised it was possible. 'I guess I could discuss it with Soph and Bella. I've always believed they incorrectly assumed that our parents found all of us wanting. But maybe that wasn't true.

'In any case, I *do* want to let it go. That stuff has no part in my future, except for me to learn from it and choose to be a better person than either of my parents was.'

'So let it go with me.' His face softened, and he swallowed hard before he spoke. 'I want it all with you, Chrissy. The house in the suburbs.' His hand dropped to cover her tummy again. 'Children. *Family.* I want to stay right here and build that with you. Please, say you'll marry me.'

'I will.' Tears rushed to her eyes and she flung herself into his arms. 'I will marry you. I can't imagine life without you now, but Nate, you don't have to stay. If you hate the idea of working here—'

'Of being among the people who taught me all I know about shipping? Who were kind to me and treated me as their own?' He shook his head.

'They really are like family, Chrissy, and if I stay I get to have that, plus you and our child, plus Henry close by and your sisters for sisters-in-law. Only a fool would leave, and I've had enough of being a fool.' He hesitated. 'Unless you have a hankering to travel?'

She pushed her owlish glasses up her nose, then on a spurt of defiance tugged them off. 'Maybe one day. For now I'd rather start that life with you right here. What about Paul Erickson? You promised him a job.'

'He'll have to accept that I'll be overall manager, but, if he's still willing, we'll share the work. I'd like to have someone there who really knows his stuff, and Erickson does.'

'That sounds like a plan.'

He smiled. 'Only part of the plan. You see, I want to be able to spend time with my wife.' His face became thoughtful. 'If you want to keep working, will you go part-time and move up? Work on the more managerial stuff? A lot of your talent is wasted where you are now.'

'Are you sure you're not saying that because you don't want me working with the handsome and appealing Mr Erickson?'

'How do you know…?' He broke off when he realised she was teasing him.

She twirled her glasses in her hand. 'Oh, I think I have a few ideas about you, Mr Nate Barrett.'

He took her glasses from her and tossed them onto the sofa. 'OK, but I want you to take the change of job.'

'If it means I get to work with the boss,' she grinned, 'I will.'

He returned the grin. 'So, no barriers remaining between us, hmm? Just how much do you need those lenses, anyway?'

'Not much.' She stifled a smile. 'In fact, the last two times I've visited the optometrist, I've had a hard time convincing her to give me even the lightest prescription. Whatever small problem I had with my eyes as a teen, it's fixed itself. I was just hiding behind them, for the most part.'

A rather hungry smile crossed his lips. 'Maybe just reading glasses, then, so I can have fun taking them off you now and again.'

Now, there was an idea. Chrissy decided she liked it. A lot.

On the same note, she pulled the pins from her hair and let it fall around her shoulders. 'Maybe I should get this cut, too. A short bob, or something. Although I'm only just starting to get used to the idea that I kind of like my hair. My mother didn't like the curls, you see, or the colour, or pretty much anything about it. But did you know it feels quite sensual when it's down? Especially against bare skin.'

He groaned. Closed his eyes as if he was in pain, then opened them to sear her with a hungry look. 'If you want to cut your hair, if you need to do that, I won't stop you.'

'But?'

'But I think it's beautiful, and if it makes you feel sexy, you have no idea what it does to me. I've got about a thousand ways to show you, though.'

'Then I guess I'll keep it long.' She grinned, thinking of the ways she could tease him with those long locks. Thinking of the stunned expression he had shown the first time he saw it unrestrained. 'For the time being, anyway.'

'And you'll marry me and make lots more great-grandbabies for Henry with me?'

'Well, you'd have to define lots. I don't know that I'm ready for a football team.' Her smile wobbled a bit. 'Actually, I have enough trouble keeping my plants alive. What if I'm not a good mother, Nate?'

'You will be.' He said it fiercely. 'And I'll help you look after the plants, or we can take them to a plant doctor or something. There are bound to be specialists out there….'

He trailed off and his expression became even more serious. 'You're my world. If it was only ever the two of us, it would be more than I had dreamed of. I love *you*, Chrissy. I love our baby, too, but he or she is an unexpected bonus. One we'll love and care for together with any others we may have.'

'I love you, too.' Her voice dropped to a loving whisper. 'And I like the idea of being your wife.'

'I like the idea of being your husband.' He tugged her to her feet and swung her into his arms. He stopped twirling her before she had a chance to get dizzy. Smiled sheepishly. 'I don't want to upset the baby.'

One last thing filtered through her mind. And it was kind of a big thing, although not particularly important. 'Since when have you owned the overseas arm of the company?'

He looked away, avoiding her glance, and mumbled into his chin, 'Um, that would be since I left six years ago and

Henry insisted I take it over so I'd be sure of a good income and future.'

'I see.' She tapped the toe of her shoe on the ground. 'And just how good is that income? Just how rosy is that…future?'

'Well, you see, I've worked really hard at it because I didn't have anything else to fill my life, and so—'

'Nate.'

He pursed his lips and turned a rather endearing shade of *blushing man*. 'I've sort of made it a multi-million-dollar concern.'

'Oh. Is that all?' She laughed at the expression of first surprise, then relief on his face. Then her laughter faded and she cupped his face and let her love for him shine in her eyes. 'You do realise you're going to have a bit of work ahead of you in order to get Bella back on side?'

He nodded. Grinned. 'Yeah, but I get two sisters out of this. That's more than enough compensation for her hating me for a while.'

'I'm glad you're looking on the bright side.' She paused, smiled again because he was just so wonderful and she loved him so much. 'And I don't think it would be a good idea to let Sophia near you with a pair of clippers any time soon, either.'

His grin broadened. 'I'll take your advice to heart and keep my hair away from her until she simmers down.'

Chrissy played her final card. 'Joe will give you the third degree, once I tell him I'm going to marry you.'

'I don't like Joe.'

She watched him struggle.

Finally, he growled, 'But I'll try to be nice for your sake.'

Then she pressed close, laid her hand over his heart and felt her own swell with warmth and love and longing. 'Will you always resent strange men who take me out and hug and kiss me?'

'Always.' His mouth dropped to hers, and in the ravishment that followed he made it a pledge to love and cherish her forever. 'Except they won't be taking you out, because you'll be busy going out with me.'

She let her heart fill. This was right. She and Nate and their baby. They would build a life together, weather the tough times and rejoice in the good. 'I'm glad you came to rescue your grandfather after the stroke, even if I didn't appreciate your presence at the time.'

'I'm glad, too, even if you frustrated me from the moment we met.' He pressed her body to his and groaned. 'Speaking of which, I really want to take you to bed.'

Chrissy gave a mischievous smile. 'So take me to the cottage. Unless you want to go parking in the convertible and finish what we started that night of the storm?'

Nate was tempted. Oh, he was tempted! His body had a number of ideas about how he could make that particular fantasy pleasurable for both of them. But not tonight.

After shouting goodbye up the staircase and raising an eyebrow at the giggles coming from upstairs—from two mouths, not one—he hurried Chrissy outside and into his car. 'It appears that my grandfather is enjoying that crossword puzzle.'

'I can think of a few erotic things I'd like to try out with you.' She said it with an air of innocence, but Nate saw through it.

He growled. Hurried their pace. 'We'll go parking another night and we'll find our own place soon, but for now, I know of this cottage hideaway in the suburbs....'

And so they went.

EPILOGUE

CHRISSY thought it was lovely of Nate—and clever—to insist that, while Gertie was in the repair shop, she and her sisters have the convertible to drive.

Soph was inclined to forgive all after her first trip with the top down, but Nate still steered clear of her clippers, just in case.

Bella was more of a challenge. For several days after discovering Chrissy's pregnancy, Bella had done little but drink copious quantities of Chai, glare at Nate any time he came into view and sew furiously.

She did eventually condescend to drive Nate's car. And she stood on the pavement in their little group now, dressed in a brand-new, even more form-fitting midnight catsuit. They were waiting for Joe to bring the refurbished Gertie out of his repair shop for inspection.

'What's keeping Joe? I'm dying to see our Gertie again. I've missed her.' Soph gave her metallic peach hair a swish, studied the ends and glanced at her sisters with a worried expression. 'Do you *really* think this colour looks all right on me?'

'*Yes.*' They said it in unison.

Bella shook her head at Soph, then she looked at Chrissy's middle and sighed.

'Mothering you two hasn't been easy.' She proceeded to

glare at Nate's hand where it rested with some intimacy on the bottom Chrissy had now forgiven for its size.

Chrissy simply grinned.

Bella folded her arms and gave her sister a very direct stare. 'Just be aware that the baby's wardrobe will be my department.'

'Of course.'

At Chrissy's swift agreement, Bella sent Nate a further threatening glance. 'If I do the wardrobe, then I may not need to hurt you, after all.'

Nate was beginning to really enjoy Chrissy's older sister. He stifled his grin, and gave a solemn nod instead. 'I'm willing to work with those terms.'

'Good.' Some of the starch left Bella's spine.

Inside the repair shop, a familiar-sounding engine started up. They all trained their gazes on the garage's yawning front.

It pained Nate to admit it, but when Joe drove the revitalised and shining Gertie out, the car looked better than ever. Joe had done a great job on it.

Then Chrissy *oohed*, and Bella *aahed*. Joe jumped from the car, grinning, and all three sisters threw themselves on the muscular mechanic and peppered him with kisses.

Nate's charitable attitude evaporated. Air hissed through his teeth. He forced his way into the group, scattering sisters in his wake until he and Joe stood face to face.

'Thank you for taking care of the car,' he grated through clenched teeth.

Joe leaned in, pushed his chin out and met him nose to nose. 'It's always my pleasure to serve *the girls*.'

'You'll let me take care of the bill.' A demand. Perhaps an invitation to fisticuffs, if Joe was so inclined.

From her position on the pavement with her sisters, Chrissy stared at the two men, then shared a glance with Bella and Soph.

They all shook their heads.

'Should we throw a bucket of water over them?' Soph cocked one hip out and set her hand on it. 'It works for howling cats and drunks. Of course, that's at the apartment where we can run inside before the drunks realise where it came from.'

'Which part of *Chrissy and Joe are friends* is it that Nate doesn't get?' Bella asked the question with laughter in her voice. Real, genuine Bella laughter, deep and throaty and rich.

'You laughed.' Chrissy teared up. She was on hormone overload already, and it showed. At this rate, it was going to be a long nine months.

Bella's eyes filled, too. She didn't even have an excuse. 'Well, that's because I'm happy, idiot. After all, I'm going to be an aunty.'

'Now look what you've done.' Soph sniffed. 'My mascara is probably running.'

They all laughed again, and fell into a hugging mass of feminine tears and kisses and smiles.

Nate and Joe stood side by side on the pavement, staring, their aggravation momentarily forgotten.

After a moment, Joe shrugged and looked at Nate. 'They're girls. They get emotional. I can dig that.'

At Nate's uncomprehending look, he paused. Tipped his head to one side. 'You do know I'm gay, right? Genuine, card-carrying, other side of the street…?'

Nate blinked. Frowned. Felt heat creep up his neck. 'Well, yeah.' He rubbed an awkward hand across the neck in question. 'I knew that. Sure. Of course I did.' He ground to a halt.

Joe laughed. 'I get to be a godparent, by the way.'

Nate grinned back, then narrowed his eyes. 'You can be a godparent if I pay the car bill.'

Joe chewed on it for a moment. Nodded. Then a teasing glint entered his eyes. 'How many kids will there be? You planning on keeping her tied to the bed for a while, making little Barrett babies?'

'Mind your own damned business.'

Joe laughed until he cried.

Nate watched with a scowl on his face, and the three sisters watched Nate and shared a few chuckles themselves. As Joe's laughter finally wound down, Chrissy's cellphone burst out with a tinny rendition of a silly pop tune.

She pressed the button, smiling as Nate moved to her side.

The pink pearl engagement ring glinted on her finger and she stared at it mistily, remembering the night Nate had given it to her. How he had opened his heart, telling her about his childhood, about his determination to be a good parent to their baby....

She realised belatedly what was being said to her, and shrieked and threw the phone up in the air, caught it then jumped up and down, her arms wrapped around Nate.

He grabbed the phone, but realised she had turned it off. 'What on earth is it? You can't have just heard we're pregnant. We already know that. We've been to the doctor for confirmation. You've been eating the porridge and lemon juice to prove it.'

She smiled and dropped a kiss on his mouth. 'Henry's crossword puzzle got third place in the competition. He says he and Sally are working on a new one, that, um, involves rather a lot more imaginative licence and should definitely get them a first prize next time around.'

'Let's go try out some of our own imaginative licence.' Heat flared in Nate's eyes and Chrissy's world tilted just like that.

She walked her fingers up his chest, liking the idea. 'Right now?'

He grabbed her hand and headed for his car. 'Remember that piece of unfinished business we had with the car and parking and, ah, you know?'

'But it's broad daylight.' She hurried behind him, laughing as her sisters and Joe stared after them, puzzled looks on their faces.

Nate just smiled. 'So we'll improvise.' He reached into the car, pulled out a set of provisional plates and slapped them onto the appropriate parts of the convertible. 'It's your turn to drive, by the way.'

She couldn't quite keep the awe from her tone. 'You want me to drive Bentley?'

He groaned. 'Firstly, you realise it isn't one, right? A Bentley?'

She nodded. 'Yeah, but he needed a name, and this one is very compatible with Gertie, I reckon.'

'Right.' He gave a resigned shake of his head, then his expression sobered. 'You're a good driver, Christianna, and it—*Bentley*—'

He paused and tried to hide his grimace in his chin, then went on, 'Bentley is *our* car now—at least until the first of our football team is born. Then I guess we could offer him to Joe and buy ourselves something a bit roomier.'

His mouth kicked into a sexy grin. 'But for now, let's try out the car's paces. Both on the road, and off it.'

That sounded just fine to Chrissy. Except perhaps the part about getting rid of the newly named car. 'Let's keep Bentley for special occasions. You know. Wedding anniversaries, naughty weekends, that sort of thing.' She grinned at him. 'Don't you think that's a better idea?'

Nate could only agree.

SAVE UP TO $30! SIGN UP TODAY!

The complete guide to your favorite
Harlequin®, Silhouette® and Love Inspired® books.

✓ Newsletter ABSOLUTELY FREE! No purchase necessary.

✓ Valuable coupons for future purchases of Harlequin, Silhouette and Love Inspired books in every issue!

✓ Special excerpts & previews in each issue. Learn about all the hottest titles before they arrive in stores.

✓ No hassle—mailed directly to your door!

✓ Comes complete with a handy shopping checklist so you won't miss out on any titles.

Introducing…

nocturne™

**a dark and sexy new
paranormal romance line
from Silhouette Books.**

USA TODAY bestselling author

LINDSAY McKENNA
UNFORGIVEN

KATHLEEN KORBEL
DANGEROUS TEMPTATION

*Launching October 2006,
wherever books are sold.*

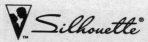

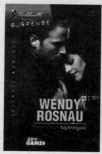

REQUEST YOUR FREE BOOKS!

2 FREE NOVELS PLUS 2 FREE GIFTS!

SILHOUETTE *Romance*®

From Today to Forever...

SILHOUETTE Romance®

COMING NEXT MONTH

#1838 PLAIN JANE'S PRINCE CHARMING—Melissa McClone

When waitress Jane Dawson approaches millionaire Chase Ryder to sponsor her charity, she is thrilled when he agrees. Deep down she knows there is no chance sexy Chase will be interested in a plain Jane like her! But Jane's passion to help others is a breath of fresh air to Chase, and he soon realizes that Jane is a woman in a million, and deserves her very own happy ending.

#1839 THE TYCOON'S INSTANT FAMILY—
Caroline Anderson

When handsome business tycoon Nick Barron hires Georgie Cauldwell to help with his property development, they spend a few gorgeously romantic weeks together. Then Nick disappears! When he returns, it is with two young children and a tiny baby. Georgie knows she shouldn't fall in love with a man who has a family, but there is something about this family she can't resist.

#1840 HAVING THE BOSS'S BABIES—Barbara Hannay

Like the rest of the staff at Kanga Tours, Alice Madigan is nervous about meeting her new boss. But when he walks through the door it's worse than she could ever have imagined! She shared one very special night with him—and now they have to play it strictly business! But for how long can they pretend nothing happened?

#1841 HOW TO MARRY A BILLIONAIRE—Ally Blake

Cara Marlowe's new TV job will make her career—as long as nothing goes wrong. So it's bad news when billionaire Adam Tyler wants the show stopped, and worse that Cara can hardly concentrate with the gorgeous tycoon around! Cara wants Adam—and her job, too. Will she have to make a choice?